Upon Wings as Eagles

COLETTE SWEERS

Editor: Kellyn Knowles
Cover Design: Outlander Marketing
Copyright © 2020 Colette Sweers
ISBN: 9798663189750

DEDICATION

To my Grandpa Jerry,
For passing on to me his love for writing.

CONTENTS

AUTHOR'S NOTE

Dear Reader,

I invite you to enter the imagination of 14-year-old me. This started out as a story I wrote just for fun as a teenager, but over the years it grew into a full-length novel. It's not 100% realistic, but it is where my imagination took me. I could have taken the time to rewrite the story and make it more realistic, but then it would have lost its charm. None of the people or events in this book are based off of real events or people. So, knowing this, let reality fade away and enter into the life of Lillian Hartley. Be prepared for adventures, laugher, heart break, and sweet friendships. I hope you enjoy the adventure!

Sincerely,

Colette Sweers

CHAPTER 1

Dear Lillian,

Where you are in the world people may say some pretty nasty things about what's happening over here. And who knows, some of it may be true. But Lillian, I want you never to forget: it doesn't matter what anybody says about the war going on over here in Vietnam; we are fighting for the freedom that the Americans have and for the citizens of these countries. If you were to just see the gratitude in the faces of these people, you'd know it is worth dying for. I don't know what will happen in the rest of my enlistment, much less the next 24 hours. But this I do know: Because Jesus loved us first, we can show that kind of love to those around us. Like John writes in John 15:13 "Greater love has no one than this, than to lay down one's life for his friends." You see that's why I'm not afraid to die for my country; Jesus gave his life for us so that we might be able to show that kind of love to others. And if that means laying down my life so that another might live then I'm willing to do it.

Love you little sis,

Jerry

"Lillian, it's time for dinner!"

"Yes, sir." I folded up Jerry's letter and climbed down from the hayloft. It was a beautiful autumn day as I came skipping out of the barn and headed toward the house. I had spent the late afternoon in the hayloft, dreaming of all the things we'd do when Jerry came home.

When I reached the house, I slipped off my riding boots and set them by the door. I went straight to the calendar--two more weeks until Jerry would be home.

"Wash up, Lil, I need to talk to you."

Dad was sitting at the table when I came into the kitchen.

"Dad, is something wrong?"

"Sit down, Lil, I need to talk to you."

I pulled out the chair and sat down. "What is it?"

He looked down at his hands folded on his plate. "I've been called up. The Marines need more men to go to Vietnam, and since I'm a reservist, they called me."

"But you can't, not so close to Jerry coming home…" It was then that I noticed my dad had been crying. He never cried; not when Mom died, not when Jerry enlisted in the Marines--never. I almost didn't want to ask the question that was lingering in the air.

"Dad is…is Jerry coming home?" My voice cracked and I could feel tears burning in the corners of my eyes.

"No, Lillian, he's not. This came while you were out in the barn." He slid a telegram across the table, but I didn't have to open it to know what it said. With shaking hands, I took the telegram and carefully opened it: Jerry had been killed in action. I stood up and headed for the front door.

Tears were burning on my cheeks as I ran out to the barn where my horse, Buttercup, still stood saddled from when I went riding earlier. Taking a handful of mane, I swung up into the saddle and rode out through the open doors.

I turned Buttercup in the direction of the cabin and let her run.

Why was the war in Vietnam doing this to us? I thought as the wind whipped through my hair. As I rode over the hills, I felt cold tears on my face. I didn't stop her until we reached the cabin; the cabin that Dad and Jerry had built years ago.

The sun was just dipping below the horizon as I tied Buttercup to the hitching rail outside the cabin and ran inside. There it was, the small, one-room cabin that was my escape from reality. There was a table in one corner and a cot in the other. I went over to the wood box and saw it was full from the last time I went out there. On a shelf on one wall were some eating utensils, along with some metal pots and pans. If I was going to spend the night, I needed to get a fire going. I went out and unsaddled and ground-tied Buttercup. I took my saddle and saddlebags inside and set them on the bunk bed, then took the box of matches from the shelf and began to build a fire. Once I had a good size fire going, I took the pot and walked the quarter-mile or so to the river to fetch some water for dinner.

After returning to the cabin, I took the venison jerky from my saddlebag and put it in the boiling water. It took a while for the venison to cook, so I made up my cot and set the table for one. The sun was going down as I lit the gas-burning lamp and set it in the center of the small table. Taking the picture of Jerry that I kept in my saddlebag, I looked at it longingly and placed it in the middle of the shelf on the wall. I sat looking at him in his Marine uniform, standing against an American flag. I wanted to turn around and see him standing in the

3

doorway with his arms out to me. Just two weeks more and I would have been able to spend a few days with Jerry out here. I turned around and saw the dark, closed door. I guess I thought that if I wished hard enough then it might come true. The crackling of the fire was joined by the sound of my walkie-talkie.

"Lillian, this is Dad. Come in, Lil."

I turned and looked at the saddlebag from which the noise was coming. Part of me wanted to go and answer him, but I decided to leave it be. By then the venison was done, so I used a hot pad to take it off the hook over the fire. Using the knife and fork, I fished the venison out and flopped it on my tin plate to cool. My walkie-talkie rang again but, as before, I let it go.

After dinner, I rinsed my dishes with some water and propped them on the hearth to dry. I spent hours that evening just lying on the cot and staring into the fire dreaming.

I must have gone to sleep, since the next thing I knew the sun was shining on my face through the small window. The fire had burned down to ash and the cabin was cold. I knew my dad would skin me alive if I was gone too long, so I packed the few things I'd brought with me and saddled up Buttercup.

The morning air was crisp as I rode over the rolling hills toward home. There was smoke coming from the pipe that served as the outlet for our woodstove. I rode up and headed straight for the barn. After I'd given Buttercup fresh water and oats, I took my saddlebags and headed inside. Opening the front door I called out, "Good morning, Dad, did I miss breakfast?"

He was sitting leaning over the kitchen table with

a cup of coffee in his hands. He looked up at me, and I'll never forget the look of weariness in his eyes.

"Young lady, you've got some explaining to do. I spent half the night looking for you, and I called you on your walkie-talkie at least half a dozen times and there was no response. Well?"

He only used "young lady" when I was really in for it. "Well, I rode over to Jerry's cabin. I needed to be alone to sort things out."

"Young lady, you're in deep trouble. You took off without saying a word to me, and you refused to pick up the walkie-talkie."

"I'm sorry, Dad, I just…"

I dropped my eyes to the floor, not wanting him to see the amount of hurt in my eyes. At that, his tone softened.

"I know, Lil, it's alright. I know how hard it is, losing both your dad and brother at the same time."

"Two more weeks, Dad! Two more weeks and Jerry would be home and safe. Why? Why now?"

"I can't answer that, because I don't know." He stood up, came over to me, and wrapped his arms around me. The tears stinging my cheeks soaked in to Dad's shirt as he held me close. "I know it's hard, Lil, but we'll make it somehow."

CHAPTER 2

The next day a woman came to pick me up and take me to the family I'd be staying with while my dad was gone. When we pulled up at the house, she stopped the car and we got out.

"Lilly, this is the Johnson family; you will stay with them for now while your father is away."

With that, I put out my hand to shake. "Nice to meet you, Mr. Johnson. I'm Lillian Hartley."

"Good to meet you too, Lillian. This is my family: my oldest, William, who is fifteen, followed by Laura, who is thirteen, and last but not least, my dear Amber, who is ten."

Then he turned to one of his daughters. "Laura, would you please take Lilly and show her where her bedroom will be?"

"If you don't mind, I'd prefer to be called Lillian, Sir."

"Alright, Lillian, you can go with Laura."

I followed her into the house. As we entered, I looked around and thought about this house being my new home.

Halfway up the stairs, she turned to me. "Do you like school? I'm a straight-A student."

"I don't know, never been."

I will never forget the shocked expression on her face. "You have never been to school! How old *are* you?"

"Fourteen."

"And you have never been to a day of school in your life?"

"Sure, I went to a Sunday school when I was really little, but that's about it."

"So, you don't know anything. Right?"

"I know plenty. Every evening after the dinner dishes were done, we would clear the table and get out our books. My dad would teach my older brother and me how to read, write, and do pretty much any story problem in math he could come up with."

"What about the other stuff, like science, and history, and social studies?"

"I know a little history, and my dad taught me all about how animals run. But I don't know anything about social studies. But my dad taught my brother and me-- mostly me, though--about the military and its purpose."

Just then, Mr. Johnson called for us to hurry and come down to the kitchen when we were done putting my stuff away. Laura led me the rest of the way up the stairs, down a short hall, and into a bedroom.

"Well, this is our bedroom now; you can put your backpack on that bed over there, then let's go down to the kitchen as Dad told us to. Oh, and I suggest you don't say anything about never going to school before."

We went downstairs and into the kitchen, where Mr. and Mrs. Johnson were sitting. Mr. Johnson asked me to sit down; we needed to talk.

"Now that your father and mother are gone, you are in our care, Lillian. Tomorrow being Monday, we will

7

enroll you in school. Laura, maybe you could show Lillian some of your books, or maybe the nail polish you got last weekend."

"No thanks, I'm going to go out back and get some fresh air instead."

I went out the back door into the yard. Then I saw William chopping wood. I watched him a minute and could tell he was tired. "You want a hand?"

"You? Chop wood? But you're a…"

"I'm what?" I couldn't help but crack a smile.

"You're a *girl*."

That just made me laugh. "Does that mean a girl can't swing an ax?"

"No, but…"

"Here, I'll show you."

"Okay, but if you hurt yourself, I'm telling Dad I had nothing to do with it. You don't even want my gloves?"

"No thanks, I've worked on a ranch all my life. I've got working hands."

I chopped wood for a while as he sat and watched. As I glanced over to him between swings of the ax, I saw his expression turn from a look of a shock that a girl could chop wood to a look of respect that a girl had the muscle and the will power to chop wood.

"You must be the only girl who can chop wood and enjoy it."

"Hey, what can I say? I'm a rancher through and through."

After I got a fair amount chopped, I put down the ax so Will and I could stack it in the woodshed. We had barely got started when Mrs. Johnson came out.

"Lillian, you should go upstairs and get acquainted with Laura. I think you'll find you have much in common."

I gave Will a look, seeing if he could get me out of this. He just shrugged as if he was saying, "What can I do?", so I wiped my hands on my jeans and went upstairs. When I got to the room, the door was open; however, I knocked on the door frame anyways. Like my dad used to do.

"Come in." She was sitting at her desk typing away on her typewriter.

"Hi. Your mom said I should come up and play with you."

"Sure, just let me finish up this paragraph."

That was the first real time I looked around the room. She had a poster of someone who I guessed was a singer on one wall. On another, there was a bookshelf full of books that I didn't recognize. And there was a plastic box with little bottles that had different colored liquids in them. I reached up, took one out of the box, and looked at it.

What on earth would you use this for? I thought. I turned to Laura, who still had her nose in her typewriter. "What's this?"

She barely looked up. "Nail polish."

"What's it for?"

"You put it on your finger and toenails to make them look pretty."

"Oh, okay. What do you want to do?"

She'd put her typewriter away and was sitting on the edge of the bed. She looked around.

"We can listen to music. Do you like *Nancy Drew*?

I've got the whole series if you want to read some."

"No thanks, I haven't heard of those books."

She looked at me skeptically for a minute as if she didn't believe me. "Well then, if you don't read *Nancy Drew,* what do you read?"

"History, when I have time. The ranch work and my school keeps me pretty busy."

We sat on the bed listening to the radio and looking at her books, nail polish, and other things like that for what felt like hours. Within fifteen minutes, I wanted to leave. I could tell we had nothing in common; what I wanted to do was to go out back and stack wood with Will, while all she wanted to do was listen to the radio and paint her nails. I was saved by a voice from downstairs. "Lillian, Laura, time for dinner."

It was Mr. Johnson calling us to dinner. I looked out back and saw Will take off his gloves and start toward the house. We went down to the dining room and gathered around the table. After we began eating, Mrs. Johnson asked me, "So, Lillian, what do you like to do for fun?"

"Horseback ride, mostly."

"Oh, do you take riding lessons out in the country?"

"No, ma'am, I have a mare by the name of Buttercup. I kinda have to, to work on the ranch with my father. We were planning a couple of day ride, but then life got in the way."

"Oh, before the accident happened that killed your father?"

"No, ma'am," my eyes dropped to my plate, "before my dad was called up to go to Vietnam. He's a US

Marine reservist."

Hearing that, Mr. Johnson turned to me and said, "Lillian, there's something we need to get straight. In this family, we don't praise war like some do. To us, what's happening in Vietnam and Southeast Asia is the work of the devil. This family believes in peace and love, so if you're going to live here, you're going to accept those principles or pay for it. Is that understood?"

What I wanted to do was stand up and say I wouldn't accept it, but I knew from experience that talking back to an adult just got you more trouble. So instead I said as calmly as I could, "Yes, sir."

I realized that the Johnsons didn't know what happened to my dad; since Miss Margret just said he was gone, they assumed he was dead. Dinner went on without a word, and as soon as I was done, I asked if I could be excused. They said that I could, so I went upstairs, got the bridle I was working on, and went and sat down on the back steps to work on it. After a while, Will came out and sat down beside me.

He watched me for a minute. "What are you doing?"

Without looking up, I said, "Using different kinds of weaves to make this bridle out of strips of cowhide for my horse."

Then I thought of a question I needed to ask him.

"Will, there's something I need to ask you if I'm going to start school. What does H2O stand for?"

"What kind of girl are you? You can chop wood better than I can, you don't like anything that normal teenage girls like, you've got a mare by the name of Buttercup, you can make a bridle using only strips of cow

11

leather, and you don't even know what H2O stands for?"

Just then, all the things that had been welling up inside me for the past six hours went out of me.

"No, but to answer your question, I'm a girl whose mother died from influenza when she was six. I'm a girl whose brother ran away to join the military and was later killed in the war. I'm a girl who has never been to a day of school in her life. I'm a girl who has spent her entire life on a ranch and is a rancher through-and-through. I'm a girl whose entire life was shattered by one phone call calling my dad out of Marine Reserves to active duty. I'm a girl who was taken from her ranch and put in a suburb home while her dad was sent off to one of the most dangerous places in the world. I'm a girl who feels like an eagle with a broken wing."

We sat there for a minute in silence. I was looking down at the bridle in my hands.

Will broke the silence. "'Mount up on wings as eagles.'"

That made me smile. "The prophet Isaiah wrote that."

I decided right then and there that I was going to try to live by those words. I had Will and faith in Christ Jesus on my side. Nothing had changed about my life. My mother and brother were still dead, my father was still going off to war, and I still didn't know what H2O stood for. But I had a new strength now, an inner peace I'd never experienced before. Which reminded me. I turned to Will.

"Will, you still haven't answered my question, what *does* H2O stand for?"

He laughed. "Water."

"Oh, okay. Thanks."

After a while, Mr. Johnson called us in and told us half an hour until bedtime and an hour till lights out. We went in, and I went upstairs to the bedroom I now shared with Laura. She was lying on the bed reading when I came in. Without looking up, she asked, "Where have you been? Haven't seen you since dinner."

"Out on the back steps."

I grabbed my pajamas out of my backpack and headed to the bathroom to change. Mr. Johnson stopped me in the hall.

"Lillian, we will be enrolling you in school tomorrow morning, so we will need to know if you were in any honor classes at your old school."

I had no idea what those were, however, since I had never been to a real school. "No, sir."

"Did you take any advanced learning courses?"

"No, sir."

"You didn't skip any grades?"

"No, sir."

"Alright, so what were your grades like?"

"I don't know. My father would grade my work, then write it down in a notebook of his. He didn't tell me my exact grade, he just helped me to learn the material. Excuse me, sir, I need to use the bathroom while it's open."

I left him with a confused expression on his face. I had dropped a hint that I was homeschooled, but he didn't know what to make of it. I got changed and went to bed. I lay awake thinking and wondering what school would be like. Finally, I drifted off to sleep.

CHAPTER 3

I was up at the crack of dawn. The house sounded so empty and quiet. I slipped into my clean pair of jeans and a t-shirt, took my bridle from my backpack, and tiptoed down the stairs. The sun was just throwing its first beams into the sky as I sat down on the back steps to work on my bridle and watch the sunrise. It was a brisk morning, and I was glad I had grabbed my leather jacket before leaving my room. I hugged it around my shoulders, took a deep breath of the crisp fresh air, and looked up at the sky. How beautiful it was, as the sun was just cresting over the hills beyond. With the birds beginning to chirp their morning song, the leather jacket wrapped around my shoulders, and the bridle in my hands, for a few minutes it made me feel as if I were … home. It reminded me that things might be a tornado around me, changing every second; however, there's one thing that will never change: the beauty of God in nature no matter where you are.

My peace and quiet were interrupted by a voice from inside. "Lillian, come in before you catch a cold. You are going to a new school today, and the last thing we want is for you to go there with the chills because you stayed out too long in the cold."

It was Mrs. Johnson calling out the back window.

I must have been out there for quite a while, since the sun was already high in the sky. Funny how it is; it felt like just a minute when it must have been at least forty-five minutes or an hour. After I went inside, I asked if I could help put breakfast on the table, but Mrs. Johnson said just to go upstairs and get ready for school. I thought I already was, though I went upstairs hoping to run into Will. We ran into each other in the upstairs hall. Before he could go around me, I asked him, "Will, what's school like? Will you be there to back me up?"

"No, I won't be going to your school. However, I will be walking with you, Laura, and Amber to school. You see, from here we walk Amber to her school, then about five blocks beyond that is where you and Laura go to school, and then across the street from your school is mine."

"That's a lot of schools for not very many people."

"Oh, there are plenty of people around here once you get to know the area. You'll get used to it. Besides, as soon as the let-out bell rings, I come over to your school to meet you and Laura, then the three of us walk to get Amber, then the four of us walk the rest of the way home together. It will be fun, trust me."

"If you say so."

At that moment, Mrs. Johnson called us down to breakfast. We all gathered around the dining room table and had breakfast, then it was off to school. Laura said just to follow what she did and it would be a breeze. All the way there, I wondered what it would be like. I was soon to find out. We dropped Amber off at her school, then continued on to our own. I had only three things to take to school, though Laura insisted for me to take my backpack. I had my sticks of chalk and slate that I'd been using as long as I could remember, my writing notebook, and a book of story problems and math drills my dad had me working in. I didn't see why I needed it when I had so little; however, Laura told me I would really need it by the end of the day.

We said goodbye to Will in front of our school. Laura said we needed to hurry, since this was my first day here and her dad had already signed me up. I followed her in the front doors and down a long hallway. She went up to a long line of metal boxes lining one wall. She opened one, took off her jacket, put it in, then turned to me and said, pointing to the box next to it, "That's your locker."

She handed me a small slip of paper and said, "Here's the combination; memorize it, then tear it up and throw it away. Put your jacket in your locker, then follow me to our first class."

I did as she said. When we got to our classroom, we filed in with some other kids. The teacher was sitting at her big desk in front of a whiteboard; I'd seen them advertised in the paper, but my family always used a chalkboard. Laura said to stand by the teacher's desk, and when she looked up, to tell her who I was. Meanwhile, she went to her own desk. I stood there for a minute till she looked up.

"Yes?"

"Hello, ma'am, I'm Lillian."

"Oh, yes, you're the new girl. Well, Lillian, do you have any of the textbooks yet?"

"No, ma'am."

"Alright then, here are the ones we are studying

from. You may sit in the desk in the back right."

She handed me a couple of textbooks and pointed to the desk that I would be using. I went and sat down, then read the names of the textbooks that she handed me. One was on math, one on U.S. history, and one on science. Out of the blue, a bell rang. The children who were out of their seats talking hurried back to their desks. Mrs. Stevens (that's the name of the teacher) had us all stand up and say the pledge of allegiance to the American flag. Then we sat down, and she handed out something called a pop quiz - a test that you don't know when it will be. I had no idea what the answers were. I had never heard of the questions, such as *Who was Imhotep?* or *What is Niels Bohr remembered for?* I guessed at the answers, hoping they were true. The rest of the morning was uneventful; when the bell rang every hour we would put out one set of books and take out another.

At lunchtime, we all went in to the big cafeteria. Mrs. Johnson had made our lunch, so we took our seats at one end of a long table and began to eat. While Laura talked with her friends, I spent the entire time looking out the window and at the sky beyond. Our classroom didn't have any windows, so I took advantage of this opportunity. All I wanted to do right then was run. Run out of this school, out of this town, and to my home.

The rest of the afternoon went as the morning did, till finally the let-out bell rang at about 2:30pm. Mrs. Stevens asked to talk to me after the rest of the class had left. She waited for everyone to leave, then said to me, "Lillian, there is an oral report due the day after tomorrow on your hero. These kids have had two weeks to work on it, but I think you will do fine, okay?"

17

"Yes, ma'am."

I slipped into the hall to catch up with Laura. We met Will in front of the school and started home. I told him about the pop quiz and the report I was to give. He said this was an opportunity to show them who I really was. Then I knew exactly who I was going to do my report on. The rest of the way home I was thinking of how I could go at it. We picked up Amber and she gabbed the rest of the way home about the game they played at recess and the project they did in art class.

When we got home, Mr. Johnson called to Will to fill the wood box. I told Will that if he would put my backpack in my room, I'd fill the wood box. He agreed, so I ran around back to get an armload of wood. As soon as finished that chore, Mrs. Johnson sent me upstairs to do homework. When I got to my room, Laura was sprawled out on her bed, so I took my backpack and sat down at the desk to work. I rushed to get my math and history done so I'd have time to do my favorite thing in my homework list. I took out my writing notebook and wrote at the top of the page, *My Hero: David Hartley.*

And the next hour I spent writing the report I was to give the day after tomorrow. Then, there was a knock on the doorframe. Laura came.

"Dad wants to talk to you in his den."

"Alright."

I went downstairs to his den. The door was closed, so I knocked and he said to come in. I opened the door and entered. He was sitting behind his desk, and his face told me I was in trouble. He had a few pieces of paper stapled together.

He looked up. "What is this?"

"My science pop quiz, sir."

"And what is that?!" He pointed to a big, red, circled *F* on the paper.

"An *F*, my grade for the quiz, sir."

"And why did you get an *F* on your quiz?"

"Because I didn't know the material, sir."

"And *why* didn't you know the material?"

"Because I have not learned much science except biology before today, sir."

"And why not?"

"Because, before today, I have never been to a day of real school in my life, sir."

"Explain."

"Ever since I could walk, I've worked on my family's ranch. Every evening my family would finish the dinner dishes and clear the table. Then, my brother and I would get out our books, and my mother and father would teach us. We would work for two hours every night, five days a week, spring, summer, fall, and winter. It was always the same. Until my mom died, then we worked harder. My father started keeping us at the table for three hours every night instead of two. He taught us more during the daytime, too, telling us about how Washington crossed the Delaware while we fixed a broken section in the fence, drilling us with story problems out of the blue, or teaching us the science behind animals like cows. But he never put much emphasis on other science or economics; what we learned were all things we would be able to use on the ranch. So, I never went to real school."

"Alright then, but from now on I won't take any grade below a *B*. Is that understood?"

"Yes, sir."

"You're excused."

With that, I left the room. I decided at that moment that I was going to show him I could get an *A* on my upcoming report. I only had two days to do it, but I knew my subject so well I could get it done. I went back up to my desk and made a list of everything he had done, his traits, and why he was a hero to me. The list went as follows:

Things he had done:

- Worked and earned enough money to start a ranch.
- Provided a good home for his wife and two children.
- Served his country by joining a U.S. Marine Corp Reserve Unit.
- Was a good husband to his wife until she died from influenza.
- Was a dedicated father to his five-year-old daughter and sixteen-year-old son when their mother died.
- Stood firm when his son ran away to join the military and was killed in Vietnam.
- Despite all things, when the call to arms came, he was ready to answer it. He was called into active duty just a few days ago.

Before long, Laura and I were called down for dinner. As we began to eat, Mrs. Johnson asked us how school was. Laura piped up. "We had a pop quiz in science today, and I got an *A+*."

"Well done. And what about you, Lillian?"

I just looked down at my plate and didn't answer.

"Lillian, Mrs. Johnson asked you a question. Now,

please answer her. What was your grade on your science quiz?"

I kept my eyes on my plate. "An *F*, ma'am."

Mrs. Johnson and Amber gasped, and I was pretty sure I heard a snicker come from Laura.

"For heaven's sake, why did you get an *F*?"

"Because before today, other than biology I've never studied science before."

"And why not?"

"Never been to school before. Sure, my father taught my brother and me at home; however, we learned the things we could use on the ranch, like reading, writing, arithmetic, animal biology, and a little history. Not much else."

"Well, starting now, you are going to study science, and everything else, till the lowest grade you get is a *B*+. Is that understood? Good grades are essential if you want to go anywhere in life. Just look at Laura. If she keeps her good grades up, she will be able to go anywhere she wants to for college, and even Harvard or Yale won't be able to turn her down. So, from now on, I won't have any more of this playing with leather strips to make useless bridles, because around here there are no horses to ride. Even if there were, Mr. Johnson and I would not let you till you get your grades under control. You might as well stop dreaming about horses and ranches, because that is all in the past now. Since we cannot change it, we'd best forget it and move on with our lives."

And I thought the scolding I got from *Mr.* Johnson was bad; this was plain humiliating.

"Yes ma'am, understood."

And I went back to my eating. As soon as dinner was

over, I asked to be excused. I ran out the back door and sat down on the back steps with my head in my hands. I wasn't going to let myself cry, but she was trying to take away the last thing I had left of my real family: my memories.

As I sat there, they all came back to me. The time my dad first taught me how to ride a horse. How my brother taught me how to braid and do other weaves to make ropes, and eventually a bridle. How my mom used to read to us after our books were put away at night, and how Jerry and I used to ask her to read "Just *one* more chapter," or, "Please, Mom, one more page." Most of the time, she would just send us off to bed. And her and my dad would stay up talking long after we were asleep. However, every once in a while, she would let us stay up past our bedtime, and she would read one more chapter. That was the nice thing about Mom: she would stick to the rules down to the very letter, but, every once in a while, she would bend them just a little bit to let us by.

Then there were the long horseback rides my dad took me on after Jerry enlisted. We would be gone for hours and sometimes days. Every once in a while, we would make sure the chickens and the milk cow had enough food for three days, then we would pack our saddle bags, strap on our bed rolls, and we'd be off! We would usually go to the furthest end of our property, which had a river flowing through it, and make camp. By night we would lay under the stars, and by day we'd fish, relax, and have a good time. Then, on the morning of the third day, we would pack up camp and head home.

I was so caught up in my memories that I didn't hear the back door open, then close, and I didn't realize I wasn't alone anymore till I felt an arm around my shoulders. I turned my head and saw Will sitting there.

"Lil, you okay?"

"Don't call me that! That's just what my dad used to call me. I'm fine."

"You sure? My mom was pretty harsh. You don't look fine; come on, you can talk to me."

Seeing that look in his eyes, for the first time since my dad had left, I knew I could trust someone with what I was feeling. For the first time since Jerry left, I had a big brother who understood me, and I knew I could confide in him.

I leaned in to him and said, "I don't belong here, Will, I just don't belong. I'm the black sheep in the family; all your family cares about is how well you do in school, or if you made the honor roll, when that's not me! I'm a rancher clean through. I like to work with my hands, and to be out on the open plains herding cattle or repairing a fence that a tree fell on in the last storm. I don't like to sit still, and that's what your parents are trying to get me to do. I'll explode if I don't get out."

He put his other arm around me and drew me close.

"I'll make you a deal. Give it a couple weeks, and I won't rat on you. If you still feel this way then, you can go, and I won't say a word. However, if you take off any sooner, I'll tell them exactly where you are going and they'll be there waiting for you. Where will you go, anyways?"

"Back to our ranch. I'll get Buttercup a few more supplies, then go looking for a job, probably on a big spread that needs a lot of hands and that pays well. My father taught me all there is to know about ranching and I

23

can work just as hard as a man."

"What about family? Will you have anywhere to call home?"

"Nope, I'll live off the land. Eventually I'll settle down and raise the best beef cattle in all of Texas."

We sat there for a while in silence. The way he held me close to comfort me reminded me of the night before Jerry left; I guess big brothers are all similar in one way or another. Just sitting there with his arms around me felt so good--knowing someone was there for me, knowing someone cared. We must have sat there longer then I thought, because it felt like just a minute had gone by when Mr. Johnson stuck his head out of an upstairs window and told us that if we wanted to get our homework done before bedtime we'd better come in soon. He brushed the loose hair away from my face and looked in to my eyes. "You alright, Lillian?"

"Yeah, I am now. Thanks for understanding me, Will."

"Hey, that's what big brothers are for. Now don't forget our deal."

"Then thanks for being a big brother," I said with a grin.

With that, he got up, turned, and walked into the house. I followed him, went upstairs, and worked on my report a little more before bed. As I lay in bed, I thanked God for a big brother like Will.

CHAPTER 4

I was up with the sun and went out back for about an hour, then went back up to my room to get ready for school before Mrs. Johnson came down to start breakfast. After I got all my homework in order and my backpack ready, I headed downstairs for breakfast. Mr. Johnson stopped me in the entryway with a letter in his hand.

"Good morning, Lillian. This letter just came for you--special delivery."

I took the letter and looked down at it. It was Dad's handwriting for sure.

"Thank you, sir."

I went into the living room to sit down and opened up the letter.

Dear Lil,

How's your new home? I went to receive my orders and I found out I would be serving under a new officer. When he heard my name was Hartley, he asked me if I knew a young man by the name of Jerry Hartley. I told him he was my son. When he heard that, I saw a bit of hurt come in to his eyes. He had been there the day Jerry had died, and he said he died as a hero for his country. I'm in the battalion that Jerry was in. Lillian, Jerry did not die in vain. And I don't want you to ever think that he died anything less than an American hero. Don't forget, it doesn't matter what happens over here; as Christians we have the assurance that we will be together again in heaven.

> *Sincerely,*
> *Dad*

I folded up the letter, then got up and went to the breakfast table. I felt as if, if I thought really hard, I could still feel my dad's loving, caring arms around me. I didn't say more than two words through breakfast and on the walk to school. After Laura and I put our jackets in our lockers, she turned to me and said to follow her. Because it was Tuesday, we went to a different class first, then we had an hour of study hall. When we walked in to the classroom, I introduced myself as Lillian, and she gave me a desk so we could start the class. This was a class on how the economy ran. I knew nothing about the economy except how to buy and sell stock and meat. I tried to follow along as best as I could, but most of it was over my head. I was relieved when the bell rang and we got up to leave.

We left the classroom and went down a hall to another room, except this one had a sign on the door that said "STUDY HALL." Before we went in, Laura said that we were to work on homework in here for this hour, since we did not have a class this period. We sat down at one of the tables, and I took out a piece of notebook paper to start a letter to Dad.

> *Dear Dad,*
>
> *My new home is…hard to get used to. They have a fifteen-year-old son who is a lot like Jerry; his name's Will. Other than him, there is nothing good about this place. I know you're going to say count your blessings, and think about what you do have and not what you don't. Even though it's hard, I'll try to do it any ways, for your sake. By the way, I have to do a report at school about my hero*

tomorrow, and guess who I picked—that's right, a man by the name of David Hartley (that's you, Dad.) One thing I still do have that I look at every night is yours and Mom's wedding picture, the one where you have the big bushy beard.

Your loving daughter,

Lil

As soon as I finished my letter to Dad, the bell rang. I put my stuff away and got up to go. The rest of the morning and lunch were uneventful till the class right after lunch. Laura had an advanced learning class, so I had to go to this one alone. She showed me where the classroom was, then ran off to her own. I went in to the room, and when I told the teacher who I was, he assigned me a seat, and class began.

Then he noticed my brother's dog tags I was wearing. "Lillian, I'm going to have to ask you to take off those dog tags. In this classroom, we promote peace and love and courage, not hate, war, and cowardness."

"I cannot do that."

"And why not?!"

"Because my brother wore these proudly to his death in Vietnam. These don't represent war and hate and cowardness. Just the opposite—they represent all the young men who stepped away from their lives and joined the military to fight in Vietnam. It represents heroism and courage, honor and duty. Things that you have probably never experienced in your life."

"And what would your father say if he heard you speaking this hogwash?"

"He'd agree with me."

"Humph. Well, we'll just see about that now, won't we?"

27

"Sure, we will, if you can find him." At that I stood up from my desk. "But you're going to have to trek to the deep forests of Vietnam to find my dad, because that's where he is— doing his duty with his fellow countrymen and treading on the same ground where his son gave his life for freedom. You're welcome to go find him, but I suggest you join the Marines first."

"Those men are murderers!"

"They're heroes! They've sure got a lot more courage than you; you keep talking about peace and love, but you ignore the fact that—if we didn't have men and women giving their lives for this country, do you know where we'd be? We have a communist government telling you when to eat, when to sleep, and what to think. Is that really what you want?"

"I've had enough of this meaningless talk! Sit down this instant, or you'll be in the principal's office."

"Yes, sir."

I sat down and knew Jerry would have been proud. It was only then that I looked around—all eyes were on me as if I had done something wrong. There was a slip of paper on the desk. I turned it over and it said, "Mr. Morgan is the strictest teacher in the entire school. You are the first student in the history of the school who has had the guts to stand up and disagree with him. The word will spread like wildfire and you will be the fame of the school in no time."

I crumpled it up and shoved it in my pocket. I didn't like it that people were astonished that I would stand up for what I believed to be true. For the rest of class my head was spinning. As soon as the bell rang, I got out to the hallway to find my next class as soon as I could.

A boy came up beside me, and without turning or looking at me, he said, "You being the new girl here, Mr. Morgan went easy on you; but if I were you, even if you don't agree with what is being taught here, I wouldn't stand up to a teacher or disagree with one again. It could land you a trip to the principal's office. Trust me, I was just like you when I first came here, so I know from personal experience. By the way, I agreed with every word you said in class today, and I think you've got guts."

With that, he walked away without another word. I didn't even know his name, but I was glad for the warning. The last thing I wanted was for the Johnsons to get any more involved in my life, or to question me about exactly what I believed. The rest of school was uneventful. On the walk home I didn't say much even to Will; I was too busy thinking about free speech, how to state my opinion respectfully, and the report on my hero I would be giving tomorrow. When we got home, I went straight up to my desk to finish my report for tomorrow. I also added this idem to my list about Dad: Was added to the 27th infantry battalion of the Marines and sent to the front lines of the war in the Vietnam.

I worked on my homework and report until I was called down for dinner. Pretty much as soon as I sat down, Mrs. Johnson asked how school was. Before I could stop her, Laura piped up. "I heard in the halls that Lillian stood up and disagreed with the strictest teacher in the entire school: Mr. Morgan."

I shot her a glare across the table. The note was right; the word did spread like wildfire. Before I could speak up to defend myself, Mr. Johnson looked at me. "Is this true, Lillian?"

"Yes, sir."

"Tell us what happened."

"Mr. Morgan asked me to take off the last thing I have of my brother. He asked me to take off my dog tags. He said they represent hate and cowardness. I bluntly disagreed with him, so I did as my father taught me, and that is to state your opinion respectfully, yet clearly. I did so; however, for some reason that's frowned upon. Before I knew it, the word was out and I was the gossip of the entire school since I had done something unheard of in school."

"Lillian, I have had enough of you standing out in school in a bad way. Before long you will bring shame, not only to you, but also the people in your family, so as your father I am telling you to be a *straight A* student and to learn whatever you are asked to in school, whether you agree with it or not. Do you understand?"

I was so angry it felt like I had smoke coming from my nose. What I wanted to say was, "This isn't my family, and you're not my father, so you can't tell me what or what not to do!" then I'd storm out to the back steps and just sit there alone. Nevertheless, I knew if I did that, I'd probably get an awful bad whipping since it would be downright disrespectful. At least, that's what my father would do if I did that at home. *My father.* Those words sounded so far away, even though it was just the day before last that I'd said goodbye to him. So instead, I hid my feelings and looked down at my plate.

"Yes, sir."

I understood what he said? Yes. Did that mean I could keep to it? No, I couldn't, and I knew that. I'd been in school two days in my entire life, what did he expect?

The one thing that really bugged me about what he said was "your family," and "being your father,"; he acted as if my dad had already been killed, and I didn't like it. For the rest of diner I didn't say anything, and as soon as it was over I ran upstairs, grabbed my notebook that my report was in, and slipped out the back door, only stopping long enough to say, "I'm going to finish my report for tomorrow, call me when it's time for bed."

Then I escaped to the only place I could get away from this loony house. As I sat on the back steps, I looked down at the notebook in my hands. It was the notebook I had been writing short stories down in for years. I opened up the front cover and looked at the picture I had of Jerry in his Marine uniform against an American flag. I took the picture of Dad that he'd sent me in his letter this morning from my pocket and placed him next to Jerry. They were almost identical; however, Jerry had my mom's eyes, deep sea green; but me? I had my dad's, true blue all the way. The back door opened. I didn't have to turn to see who it was, and there was only one person who would follow me out to the back steps.

"You can't write a report without your pencil, you dropped it on the way out here. Something on your mind? You've hardly said two words to me all day," Will said as he sat down beside me.

"Isn't there always?"

"That's five words. What's bothering you this time?"

"In the letter from Dad I got, he said he was put in Jerry's battalion."

"That's not all, is it?"

"No. He said he talked to the sergeant that Jerry

31

was under. The sergeant said Jerry was a hero, an American hero. Then, at school, the teacher said that the men fighting in Vietnam were murderers and cowards. Then—I couldn't take it, Will; I disagreed with him and told him what I believed. Well, he didn't like it. The whole class acted as if they didn't know how to stand up for free speech. So much for free speech. Are you sure you won't shorten our agreement to Sunday instead of a couple weeks?"

"Lillian Hartley, if you're anything like the girl I think you are, you'll keep our agreement because you gave your word. Come on, it won't be so bad. All you need is a little perseverance. Anyway, you give that report tomorrow, right? That's the place where you can state your opinion on what a real hero is without anyone to stop you."

"Okay. I'll stay, for a couple more weeks."

"Good."

That night when I went to my room right before bed, I added this to my letter to Dad:

P.S Don't write to me at this address again, I might not be here long enough to receive your next letter. When I settle down for good, I'll write to you with the address that you can write to me at

Then, I turned out the light and went to sleep.

CHAPTER 5

The instant I woke up I was excited for the day to come. Today was the day I was going to give my report. The entire way to school I went over my report section by section. When we reached school, we went into class and Mrs. Stevens told us what order we would be giving our reports in—I got to go last. A lot of the reports I heard were about famous people or people who did great things. Therefore, when I got up to speak, the class was in for a surprise.

Throughout the entire report I hadn't told them that he was my father, so that's why my favorite part was the very end, when I finished off by saying, "That's why my father, David Hartley, is my hero."

That's how I ended it; it was great, the best I could have ever hoped to do. However, the best part was when at the end of class our teacher handed out the grades for our reports. I looked down at the write-up she did on my report, and in the middle of a red circle there was a big $A+$. I couldn't wait to write my dad and tell him how I did. When we were outside waiting for Will to get out, I thought about how Dad would feel when I told him I actually got an $A+$. As we started to walk home with Will, I told him all about my report. I could tell he was happy I had done so well, and I think he was hoping that might mean that I'd stick around a little longer. And who knows? Maybe I would. When we got home, I almost skipped up the stairs.

Mrs. Johnson stopped me at the top and asked, "Lillian, I heard you had an oral report due today. How did it go?"

"Good. I got an *A+*, ma'am."

"That's good to hear."

Then I escaped to the desk in Laura's and my room. I quickly took out a piece of notebook paper and started it.

Dear Dad,

I was about halfway through when Laura came in. "You really should get to your math homework. We have a lot, and the teacher is really picky if we don't get it all turned in on time."

I knew she was right, so I put my letter aside and took out my math. Finally, when I finished my agonizing math homework, I went on to social studies. Soon enough I was called down for dinner. As I sat down at my spot at the table, I tried to act as if everything was normal. As soon as dinner started, Mr. Johnson asked, "How was school today?"

Laura responded by saying, "Great. Lillian did a really good report on her hero."

"Oh, really? What was your grade?"

Without much enthusiasm, I said, "An *A+*, sir."

"Good job, that's what I like to hear. Who was your hero, by the way?"

"My father, David Hartley, sir."

He smiled, and I could tell he liked my choice. I didn't talk to Will that night; instead, I went upstairs and busied myself with homework until bedtime.

CHAPTER 6

Over the next couple of weeks, I fell into a rhythm. I didn't like my teachers much but did the best I could to stay out of trouble. I decided that I might be able to tolerate living with the Johnsons until my dad came home. I didn't get any more letters from my dad, and I thought he must just be busy, until I came from home from school one day.

A man from the telegraph service was standing on the front porch with a clipboard and telegram. The man turned to me and said, "Are you Lillian Hartley?"

"Yes, sir"

"I need you to sign this, Miss," he said, handing me the clipboard.

I signed where he asked me to, but I didn't want to know what was coming next. I handed him the clipboard and he handed me the telegram.

"Good day, miss."

I had a sickening feeling growing in the pit of my stomach as I unfolded the telegram. I saw the typed print and two lines stood out to me: *David Hartley. Missing in action.*

When I turned back toward the stairs, I saw Will standing at the top. I headed back to my room, but when I got to the top of the stairs Will stopped me.

"You okay? I heard about your dad."

"I'm fine," I responded, trying not to let my voice crack.

I walked back to my room and tried to do my math homework. I found it hard to concentrate, so after a while I took out my journal.

Dear Journal,

It's finally happened. My nightmare I had when I was little has come true. A telegram came today: my dad's been reported missing in action. That means it looks like I'm going to make a living for my own. I've made up my mind. I am going to run.

The rest of dinner was uneventful. I didn't feel like talking, though I should have probably told them about my father if they didn't already know. But right now I didn't want to talk to anybody, not even Will. So, as soon as dinner was over, I went upstairs and grabbed my saddle bags and my cherry wood box, then headed to the back yard. But I didn't stop on the back steps; I went around to the back of the woodshed and sat down on an old stump so nobody could find me.

My heart hurt as it did right after my mom died and when the men came and told us about Jerry. I opened my cherry wood box and took out the leather bracelet that Jerry had given me when he went away. It said on it, *they that wait upon the Lord shall mount up on wings as eagles…*

I gripped it and remembered the last night we had together. I was sitting on the back steps when he came up beside me and sat down. That was when he gave me the bracelet. We didn't say much that night; just being with him meant so much. However, I never got that with dad— it seemed like everything happened so fast.

I put the leather bracelet back and picked up a

small, sliver, heart-shaped locket that my mom had given me on my sixth birthday, within a month of when she died. I didn't have to open it up to know what was inside. There was a piece of a flower petal from when we picked flowers together that day. On one side there was a picture of my mom, and on the other, there was a picture of my dad.

I put the locket back and took up a piece of cow leather with our ranch's brand of an eagle with an *H* on the wing, which was the brand that was on all of our cows. I put the piece of leather back and took up the little strip of rope that had all the different kinds of weaves that I learned to make my bridle out of—it was the first one I did on my own. I fingered each section one at a time, remembering how long it took to make such a short section, doing it over and over again until I finally got it right. Every time I felt like putting it down and giving up, my brother would always would encourage me to keep going until it was finally done.

I didn't realize how much I missed ranch life: riding on Buttercup, herding cattle, feeling the wind in my face. Then I picked up one of my most treasured belongings. It was my mother's wedding ring. I remembered when she had given it to me—I'd been sitting by her bed when she slipped it off her finger and handed it to me. As I remembered, I griped it tight in my hand, then slipped it onto my ring finger. There were rubies placed in a cross on a gold band, and on the inside, there was engraved "Isaiah 40:28-31," my family verse. I slipped it off my finger and put it back in my box. I hadn't noticed until I looked down and saw a puddle of tears in the dry dirt at my feet. I was jerked out of my world of memories when I heard somebody calling my name.

"Lillian, Lillian, where are you? Come out, I just want to talk to you. Listen, I know what happened, and you don't have to pretend it doesn't hurt. You haven't even looked me in the eye since we got home from school, much less talked to me. Well, since I know you're out here and I can't make you come out without a warrant for your arrest, I'll be inside. I'll be in my room if you need me."

The thing I wanted to do most was to come out and talk to Will. But instead, I started making plans, plans to run away. It was Thursday, and I had a deal with Will that I wouldn't leave till Sunday. That means I had two full days to plan my route. I sat outside, working out everything in my mind. So, it was settled. I'd leave before the crack of dawn, then I'd follow the map I had back to our ranch. From there, I would get whatever supplies I would need, take Buttercup, and go looking for work.

Now that my dad was gone, I couldn't wait any longer to start making a living for myself. Once I made enough money, I would go back to our ranch and raise the best open range beef cattle in all of Texas. My dad had taught me everything I needed to know about ranching, from cleaning out the stalls, to brushing down the horses, to herding and branding cattle. I couldn't wait to get home and go rabbit hunting with my rifle, or fishing in the river that ran through the far end of our property before I headed out to go looking for a job on a ranch somewhere. I took a piece of paper out of my pocket and started to making a list of what I'd leave behind. After I had made the list, there was only one thing I was sad about leaving at this place. That was something no one could replace, and that was my friendship with Will; the way he was being a big brother to me even though no one asked him to. After a while the sun started to go down, and I was getting tired and started to drift off to sleep. I tried to stay awake, but before I knew it, I was sound asleep.

CHAPTER 7

I woke up with a chill. Someone had put a blanket around my shoulders, and my cherry wood box was still at my feet with my saddlebags. I listened to the silence as the sun came up. When the sun was up a little, I picked up my stuff and headed inside. I tried to cover up my sleepiness as I headed upstairs.

I was quiet throughout breakfast, and on the whole walk to school, I didn't say a word. I was busy thinking about how I would run and where exactly I'd go. In our first class, the teacher said we were to write a one-page report about something we had learned for tomorrow. Today we had second-hour study hall, so when the bell rang, we went to study hall. I took out a fresh piece of paper. I stared at it for a while, then I took out my backpack and took out my journal to look for inspiration. I flipped open to a page and these words starred me in the face: *The last words Jerry said to me: "Never forget, freedom is not free."* I remembered Jerry's letter, the one I'd been reading on the day that the telegram came. I didn't understand what he'd meant when I first read that letter, but then

40

something occurred to me., I wrote at the top of my page, "The Importance of Patriotism."

When the bell rang, I wasn't done yet, so I folded it up and put it away in my backpack so that I could finish it when I got home. The rest of the day I couldn't keep my mind on my school work; no matter much I tried, my mind kept drifting.

On the walk home from school, I hardly said two words to either Will or the other two girls. I was thinking about my report, how I'd run, and what would happen to me next in my life. When we got home, I went directly upstairs, got out my half-written report, and continued to write. Thoughts kept flowing into my mind on how I could make my report better.

At last, I was done. I couldn't wait to see what my teacher would say about it. Writing my report got me thinking about my ancestors on my mom's side: how my great-grandfather fought in World War I and came home to tell about it; how my grandfather fought in World War II and came home. Now, years later, my father was carrying on our military heritage through the Marine Corps Reserve. The difference was that he didn't come home. Now I was carrying it on by writing my report about what I thought our duty was as Americans.

I did the rest of my homework quietly and did my chores without a word to anyone. At dinner, when someone asked me a question, I replied with a simple "yes" or "no." As soon as dinner was over, I went upstairs, got my notebook, and sat down behind the woodshed where I'd escaped to the night before. I opened up my notebook to a fresh page and began to write a short story.

It seemed like it didn't matter how I was feeling or

what was on my mind; I could always write short stories and clear my mind. I couldn't wait to be out on the open range where I didn't have to sit behind woodsheds to be able get away from people. Now I had something to look forward to: working on a ranch somewhere, being able to show the world what I was really made of. As I sat there, the words of a song that my dad use to sing drifted into my mind.

> *Oh, give me a home where the buffalo roam,*
> *Where the deer and the antelope play,*
> *Where seldom is heard a discouraging word*
> *And the skies are not cloudy all day.*
> *Home, home on the range*
> *Where the deer and the antelope play;*
> *Where seldom is heard a discouraging word*
> *And the skies are not cloudy all day.*

I thought about how that's what life on a ranch was for me, a place where I could be myself, not having to worry about grades or what other people thought. To me, a ranch was my home on the range, somewhere I could be free, riding over the hills and being among the cattle. After a while, I headed inside. As I walked up the stairs, I got to thinking, "What would Dad do in my shoes?" When I would ask my dad what he did when he needed help and there was no one there to give it, he would always say, "I wait upon the LORD and mount up on wings as eagles." What he meant was when you rely on God and trust that he would get you through it, you can mount up on wings as eagles. I was going to do just like my dad said. I was going to mount up on wings as eagles. I was going to act the same way as I did before I got the phone call, like nothing ever happened. On the outside I would be the same, but on the inside, I'd be figuring out how to live without my dad. When I got to my room, Laura was on her bed as usual, so I took out my patriotism report to look over. Then I read till I fell asleep.

CHAPTER 8

I woke up in the wee hours of the morning. As my eyes adjusted to the darkness, I could hear Laura's breathing. As quietly as I could, I drew my legs out from under the comforter. I'd changed into my clothes the night before, after everyone else was already in bed. Right beside my bed I had my riding boots. In the still night air, I slipped my feet into my boots and laced them up. I reached down to the end of my bed and took hold of my leather jacket that was lying there. After I slipped it on, I reached my hand under my bed where I had stowed my saddlebags.

Like a shadow, I slipped across the floor, my eyes searching the darkness for any movement as I listened for sound from anywhere in the house. Silently I slipped down the hallway and down the stairs. I was in the entryway. I took a couple more steps and I was at the door. I felt around till I found the dead bolt. Slowly but surely, I turned it until it gave the quietest *click*. Now all I had to do was turn the doorknob and I'd be able to fly, fly like an eagle. Slowly I moved my hand down and took a firm hold of the doorknob. One turn and I'd be free.

But before I had the chance to do it, a big hand curled around my hand with a firm grip. A low stern voice came from behind.,

"Let go of the doorknob, put your saddlebags down, take off your jacket and boots and leave them on the ground, then walk up the stairs and go to bed."

Busted. I couldn't see his face, but I could tell by his voice that he meant no nonsense. I figured I'd be best off just doing what he said and not even trying to argue. I did what he told me to without a word.

As I walked up the stairs with heavy steps, I couldn't help but wonder what I was in for when I got up in the morning. I slipped my hand down into my jean pocket where I had put the piece of leather with my family's brand on it. I traced the outline of the eagle, thinking about how I was an eagle with a broken wing. As I slipped back into bed, it took me a while to go to sleep. When I finally got to sleep, I had a dream where I was an eagle. I was flying in the sky, higher, higher, and then suddenly something hit me, and I began to circle down with a broken wing.

Then I was awake. I turned over and saw the clock: 7:00a.m. I figured I'd best get up, even though the last thing I wanted was to face Mr. Johnson after last night. I reached down to get my jacket from the bed post when I remembered he'd taken it the night before.

I came downstairs. Will saw me and said, "You okay? You look tired."

"Yeah, I'm alright."

"Good. It's time for breakfast."

Mr. Johnson wasn't at breakfast, and we ate in silence. I kind of got caught up thinking Mr. Johnson might have forgotten about what happened altogether.

Laura said at the end of breakfast, "Oh, Lillian, Dad wanted to talk to you in his den after breakfast."

45

I got up from the table and walked to the den. The door was closed, so I knocked. A voice within said, in the same tone that it had earlier that morning, "Come in."

I entered the room and took a quick glance around. It looked normal, except for one thing. My belongings were leaning up against a bookshelf in the corner. The look on Mr. Johnson's face made me feel like I was in an interrogation room. Then, from the other side of his big oak desk, my interrogator spoke.

"Well? What do you have to say for yourself? That stunt you played last night was going too far. From now on you will not try to run away or there will be severe consequences. Is that understood?"

"Yes, sir."

"Now, it's about time you go get ready for school, isn't it?"

"Yes, sir."

I left the den and headed upstairs. The morning went by in a blur, mostly because I was thinking about everything but school. However, when the class period came to turn in my report, we had a substitute. Class was normal till the end.

The bell had just rung when the substitute teacher said, "Alright, class dismissed. Oh, Lillian, I'd like to have a word with you before you go to your next class."

Oh, boy, I thought. I could see my report on top of the pile on his desk.

I wonder if he'll send me to the principal's office for doing my report on patriotism.

I walked to the front of the room and stood by his desk. He waited till all the other kids were out of the room, then picked up my report. "Do you really believe this?"

His question stunned me for a moment. What was I supposed to say? I could take a chance, say I did believe it, then risk a trip to the principal's office, or I could lie and go against everything my dad had ever taught me.

Taking a deep breath, I said, "Yes, sir, I believe every word of it."

"You also mention a boy named Jerry in here, did you know him personally?"

"Yes, sir…he was my brother,"

I said, dropping my eyes to the ground to keep him from seeing the hurt that had come into them.

"Lillian, not many people around here agree with you, but you are doing the right thing in doing your report on something as important as patriotism. I just wish where were more kids like you who know the truth and act on it."

With that, he handed me my report and dismissed me. It wasn't till I was out in the hall that I looked at my report. On it, this was written: "A+. I like your spirit, kid, keep it up."

For the rest of the day I thought about what he said. When I got home, I did my homework, and before long it was time for dinner. As soon as dinner was over, I slipped out the back door and sat down behind the woodshed to think. I took the piece of leather with our brand on it from my pocket and fingered it, planning my escape. My thoughts were interrupted by a voice from above me.

"So that's where you've been hiding."

I looked up into the face of Will.

"What are you doing?"

"Trying to plan my escape?"

"Then why don't you fly right now?"

47

"It's hard to fly when you have a broken wing. So, I just have to stick around and adjust."

"No, you don't, you can fly now."

"But how?"

"With these."

From behind the side of the woodshed he took my saddlebags, boots, and leather jacket and handed them to me.

"Now go, mount up on wings as eagles, run and not be weary, walk and not faint."

I took my things, "Alright, I will."

"Well, I'd better get in to finish my homework, and don't worry. I won't say a word."

With that, he turned and walked back around the woodshed and into the house. The first thing I did was take out a piece of paper and write a note to Will.

Dear Will,
May the road rise up to meet you.
May the wind be always at your back.
May the sun shine warm upon your face;
The rains fall soft upon your fields and until we meet again,
May God hold you in the palm of His hand.

Then I took three strips of leather out of my saddlebag and wove them together into a bracelet. I left my stuff out behind the woodshed where no one would find it, slipped up to my room, and went to bed just as I normally would, except this time I didn't go to sleep. My plan was completely different, and better. I waited until the whole house was asleep and still. I tiptoed down the stairs and around to the kitchen. The microwave clock read 11:00p.m. I screened the room for any movement, any sound, any light; I was in the clear. As silent as shadow, I crossed the kitchen, then I slowly unlocked and opened the back door. The first breath of night air hit me and my bare feet stepped out, feeling around for the step. The bare ground felt cold under my feet as I crossed the yard and worked my way to behind the woodshed. I found my saddlebags and slipped on my clean socks and boots. After I put on my leather jacket, I took the note and bracelet for Will and set them on the stump where I knew he'd look for me.

Taking one last look at the house and the life I knew I could never live, I put my saddlebags over the fence, took a firm grip on the top, swung over, and *thump*. I was on the ground; I was on the run.

CHAPTER 9

I didn't sleep that night. I knew they wouldn't start looking for me till morning, so I followed the trail behind the house to the main drag. After walking a while, I came to a street light. I stopped under it, then took out a pocket map of the city that I'd picked up at the library. In the dim light, I traced my finger along where I figured I had to go to get out of the city and on the right track back home. I took a brightly colored highlighter out of my pocket and highlighted the route I'd take to get home. After studying the map, a while, I folded it back up, put it in my jacket pocket, and started on my way.

I walked through the whole night, only stopping to duck behind a wall or fence when a car went by. When at last the sun started to come up, I stopped for a minute and took some beef jerky from my saddlebag. The piece was big, so using my knife, I carved off a slice. I stored the remainder and started on my way again. I sucked on the jerky to make it last. I was making good time, but I knew I'd have to rest soon if I wanted to make it home. I'd been walking all night and most of the morning. I was near the outskirts of the city, so I knew it'd be safe to stop and get some supplies for the trip home. I approached a drugstore and roamed the aisles till I found the things I'd need to continue my journey. I found an inexpensive canteen, some basic food, and some fire starters (matches). To pay for it, I used the emergency money I kept in the pocket of my jacket.

"Looks like you're going camping," The clerk remarked and as I purchased my items.

"No, sir, just going home."

He gave me a kind of funny look when I said that, but I just took my bag and left before he could say any more. After a few hours of walking, I reached the very outskirts of the city. I started to get that tingly feeling I used to get right before I left for a ride. After a little while longer, I was following only road for miles. It was a service road that ran parallel to the highway. Far overhead I heard a hawk cry. I looked up and saw him circling ever higher. It reminded me of the hawk I saw the day my dad had been called up. Except, this time, it reminded me that I was now free like that hawk.

Then something caught my eye. There was a looming rain cloud waiting to break, and soon enough it blotted out the sun and almost covered the sky. I knew what was coming, so I took out a pocket rain slicker I always kept in my backpack and slipped it over my clothes and my backpack. Within a couple of minutes, the cloud had broken and it was raining cats and dogs: huge drops that always found their way through my head hole. I figured that since I was getting soaked anyway, I might as well have fun. So, putting my head down and hugging my saddlebags, tight I ran! The rain was coming down so hard that it made it hard to run, but I did anyway. After a while I threw my head back, and as the rain pounded down on my face, I laughed.

I continued to walk. Before long the rain had

passed and the sun shone as if nothing had happened. I still had at least an hour and a half of sunlight left, so I didn't need to make camp just yet. As the sun began to set on the horizon and it was time to make camp, my rain slicker and clothes were all dried out. The ground wasn't touched by rain. I saw a river not far off from where I was, so I headed toward it and made camp far enough away that if there was a flash flood I wouldn't be washed away, yet close enough to fetch water from the river.

Once I'd made camp and cleared a fire ring, I headed toward the river to find fuel for my campfire. Not far from the bank there was a weeping willow, and under it there were dead limbs that must have fallen off in the last storm. They were thin and numerous, so they'd be perfect for firewood. I broke them into manageable-sized pieces, then carried an armload back to my camp. After I broke them into burnable-sized pieces, I started a fire using some kindling I found on my way. Once I had my fire to the size that I could leave it for a minute, I took my canteen (which was empty) and filled it up in the river. When I returned to camp, I took a pot I'd bought, filled it, and put it on to boil. While the water boiled, I had an appetizer of dried fruit. Once the water had come to a boil, I cut off a sizable piece of beef jerky and put it in water to make broth and soften up the beef.

Before long the beef was ready, and I took it off the fire to cool. Using the pot lid as a plate, I ate the meat and drank the broth. After I finished my dinner, I put the rest of the water on to boil for my canteen the next day. While the water boiled, I headed back the river and got an armload of reeds to use as a bed. I laid down the reeds by the camp fire as a bed. Using my saddlebags as a pillow and my leather jacket as a blanket, I laid down, watching the fire, and got caught up in my memories. They were from when I was little and Jerry was still around. The most vivid memory I had with him was the last evening before Jerry left.

I was about to knock on the door to my dad's bedroom when I heard voices. They were my dad's and Jerry's.

"Dad, I have to, for Mom's sake. I need to do something more than just live on the ranch. This way I'll be able to protect the freedom that we have in this country."

"Alright, son, I give you permission to enlist. I just have one question for you: do you, in your heart, believe that what you're doing is right?"

"Yes, sir, I do."

"Then I give you my blessing. I might just call the Marines right this minute and let them know what they're in for."

"No need, Dad, I'll be headed out in the morning. First stop: Marines recruiting office."

I turned and ran. I didn't stop till I got to the steps leading to the back porch, where I sat down and tried to figure out what this meant.

"Hey, Eaglet, weren't you going to groom down Buttercup?"

"I already finished."

Then, it just came out of me. "Is it true that you're enlisting in the Marines in the morning?!"

He sat down beside me and looked down at his hands. "Lillian, ever since Mom died, I've been thinking about enlisting."

"What I don't see is, why?"

"Because of Paul Revere, Nathan Hale, Abraham Lincoln, and all the others that have kept this country united and free. You remember when we were little, how Dad taught us about patriotism, and all the freedoms we have in this county. Now I'm able to defend the country that I've come to love so much, and I want the generations after us to have all the freedoms that we have. But in order to do that, I'll need my little eaglet standing by me all the way, so what do you say?"

"Alright, Jerry, I will."

"I leave in the morning, so I'd better say goodbye tonight."

He put his arms around me, and I just couldn't say a word. As he held me for one last time, he said, "Never forget: freedom isn't free."

He got up and I watched him go inside. That was the last time I ever saw my brother; by the time I got up in the morning he was gone. Four years later to the day we received word that he'd been killed in action. But one thing I never forgot about Jerry: freedom isn't free.

As I poured the water into my canteen, I decided that Jerry's form of patriotism was going to live on through me.

CHAPTER 10

The warmth of the sun on my face woke me up. As I stirred, I looked around and remembered where I was. The dew was heavy on the ground and the air brisk. After I at last got my fire going, I went and got more water to boil for breakfast. For breakfast, I made some instant noodles, then headed on my way. After a little while of walking, out of nowhere came a voice.

"Hello there, mind if I walk with you a ways?"

I nearly jumped out of my skin. I went for my knife I kept on my belt, but before I could draw it from its sheath, he defended himself. "Whoa, little lady, no need for that. I won't hurt you."

I inspected him a minute. He was young, from what I could see, had a kind face with black stubble, and wore a cowboy hat.

"How do I know you're a good man? How do I know that you won't attack me as soon as I take my hand off my knife?"

Then, holding up his right hand, he said, "I give you my word on my honor that I will be honorable, respectful, and won't do anything to harm you as long as you let me keep you company on your way."

"Alright, but as soon as you make one wrong move, I still have this knife and I know how to use it."

"If we're going to be walking together, to begin with, I need to at least know your name."

"It's Lillian, Lillian Hartley. And yours?"

"Tyler Davis. So, why are you walking out on this road so far away from everything?"

I explained to him why I was there. I figured it couldn't hurt, since we were the only ones around. After I was through telling him, he asked me, "How? How do you do it?"

"Do what?"

"Keep going, with your entire family gone?"

"I row."

"What? You mean like row a boat?"

"Well, a wise man once told me about a passage in Scripture, Psalm 107:23-24. That passage reads: 'Those who go down to the sea in ships, who do business on great waters, they see the works of the LORD, and His wonders in the deep.' Then he explained that as a Christian, we ought to not just sit on the beach, but that we should get in a boat and row toward the horizon and see the wonders of the Lord in the deep."

"But how do you row?"

"The man also told me that we row by answering God's call. Years ago, my older brother answered the call by enlisting in the Marines, then giving his life for another. My father answered by joining the U.S Marine Reserve after his son had been killed in action. I answered it by giving a report on my father and patriotism. Now I'm keeping my family's legacy going and rowing further toward the horizon by working on a ranch and using my talents for Him."

We walked along in silence for a while. My guess

was that he was thinking about what I'd said. After a while I asked him, "So, I've told you about what I'm doing out here, what about yourself?"

"Well, I am traveling, but I was on a mission not far from here when my horse ran away. I'm headed back to the home ranch. I guess you could say we're headed the same way."

"Do you have any family?"

"My family lives in Montana, but once I finished college, I came down here to Texas to work on a ranch."

"You like that life?"

"Yes. I write letters home and so that's how we keep in contact. Then I also go home for Christmas, since at that time there isn't much happening on the ranch."

"Did you ever think about settling down for good?"

"A couple times I did, but I figured out that being a ranch hand is the life for me."

For the rest of the day we walked together. We talked every so often, but for the most part we just kept each other company. When it came time to bunk down for the night, we found a place close to the edge of the lake. Tyler started a campfire while I took both our canteens and filled them up with lake water. I was bushed from the long day of walking, so when I returned to the campfire and Tyler volunteered to make dinner, I agreed with no second thoughts. As he made dinner, I wrote a bit in my journal, then took out the framed picture of Jerry. He wasn't smiling but he had that laughter in his eyes.

"Is that your brother?"

I had been so deep in my thoughts that I hadn't heard Tyler walk up. "Yes, his name's Jerry. He enlisted as soon as he turned eighteen."

"He sure is handsome."

We had dinner and the deal was that since he made dinner I got to clean up. That just meant I had to wash off the dishes in the lake. Since there were only two of us, I just had to wash two tin plates and some camping silverware. After I finished the dishes, I was tired, so I laid down to try to go to sleep. But I found that I wasn't as tired as I thought I was, so for what seemed like hours I lay looking up at the stars, trying to point out the constellations Jerry taught me to find. And, before long, I was in dream land.

CHAPTER 11

Over the next couple weeks that I traveled with Tyler, we took turns making breakfast and dinner. When we'd run low on supplies, we'd go in to a small town and restock. We talked a lot about our families and what we did for fun. He told me all about the ranch he worked on, and I told him about the cattle my dad and I raised. One morning, we came to a small town.

"Well, Tyler, this is where I split off. Our ranch is up there a ways." I pointed out of town toward the rolling hills.

"Lillian, it has been a pleasure traveling with you, and I hope you have success finding a job."

With that, we shook hands, and I headed out, following a single lane dirt road. I couldn't stop beaming knowing I was almost home. As I neared the house, something was different. I approached slowly, trying to figure out why something didn't feel right. Then it occurred to me. There was a truck that wasn't my dad's parked by the barn and a trampoline set up on the side of the house. Instead of going straight to the house, I walked over to the gate that led to the pasture. I hopped up on it and whistled to Buttercup; she didn't answer. This was strange; the only time Buttercup hadn't come to my whistle was when the vet was checking her out. I decided to take a chance and go into the house. I was about to unlock the door with my house key when I saw a sign I hadn't even noticed when I'd left with my dad. There was a sign leaning against the side of the door, and in big red letters it spelled out *for rent*. My dad must have put it up and I just was too busy to notice. I put my key away and knocked on the door instead.

A woman answered, "Yes? May I help you?"

"Yes, ma'am, do you know anything about this *for rent* sign?"

"Oh, yes, I've been trying to get my husband to do something with it, but we were so busy with moving in that he just didn't get around to it."

"So, you live here now?"

"Yes, honey, we're renting the place and we moved in several weeks ago."

"That furniture behind you, is that yours?"

"We're renting it, along with the house and the property. Why do you ask?"

"Just wondering."

At that moment a girl rode up to the hitching rail on Buttercup. Something inside of me lurched. I walked over to Buttercup and started to rub her nuzzle. "Hey, Buttercup, you know me, don't you girl? Yeah, that's right."

The girl had dismounted and came up to me. In a whiney voice she shot at me, "Her name is Sunshine! And she's my horse, so get your hands off her!"

It took all I had not to start a fistfight. Clenching my teeth so hard I thought my jaw would break, I walked over, picked up my backpack, and began to walk away.

Before I could get far, the woman called after me,

"Young lady, you should come back here and apologize for handling something that isn't yours."

By now I was shaking with anger. But instead of turning around and lashing out at her, I took a deep breath. "I'm...I'm sorry I touched your horse without asking. Where did you get this horse?"

"Why do you want to know? It's mine."

Keeping as calm as I could, I was about to tell her when a man strode up. "What's going on here?"

Before I could say a word, the girl piped up, "Dad, this girl is trying to take Sunshine from me."

My voice shaking just a bit, I corrected her. "I wasn't trying to take her, I just asked where you got her."

"Why would you want to know, anyways? It doesn't matter where I got her, she's still mine."

Before I could say anything, the man broke in. "Wait, you girl, what'd you say your name was?"

"I didn't," I said through clenched teeth.

"Hold on, I'll be right back, and no more fighting till I get back."

He turned and walked into the house.

"Well, tell your dad I'm sorry I had to rush off, and take care of that horse. I'd best get going if I want to make camp by nightfall."

"Okay. But next time, just ask before you touch my horse."

As calmly as I could, I turned and walked away from what used to be my home and my Buttercup. I went around the back side of the barn, slipped in an opening in the wall, and climbed up to the hayloft. From there, I was hidden, and yet I could see and hear everything that was happening in front of the house. I could see the girl

61

standing by Buttercup. I didn't know where the mom had gone, but before long the dad came out holding something.

It was time to start listening, "Allison, where did the girl go?"

"She just walked off, I guess she came to her senses, is all."

"Did she say anything about who she was or what she was doing here?"

"Nope. She just said to take good care of the horse and that she had better leave if she wanted to make camp by nightfall. Why?"

"You remember the man we talked to when we first saw this house was for rent? Mr. Hartley was his name."

"Yes."

"Well, I called the number he gave us if there was an emergency, and the man at the Marine Reserve told me that he'd been reported missing in action since over two weeks ago. My guess is that she ran away from whoever she was staying with to come home, and now that we're here she has nowhere else to go."

"So what?"

"The girl who you turned away was his daughter. See here in this picture? There's Mr. Hartley, and there's the girl who came and asked you about Sunshine. My guess is Sunshine used to be hers before she had to move."

That was the sign I needed to make my move. I slipped down from the hayloft, out of the barn, and around a hill so it would look like I was headed back toward town on the dirt road. Sure enough, before long the truck I'd seen came down the dirt road after me. I just kept walking. When the truck neared me, it pulled to a stop, and the man hopped out.

"Hey, kid, I need to talk to you before you leave. How would you like to have supper with my family and me? Don't worry about Alison, she was just worked up, being that you touched her horse without asking."

I couldn't help it. I hadn't had a home-cooked meal since I'd left the Johnsons.

"Alright, I will."

I got in the passenger side of the truck, and we drove back to the house. Supper was just being set on the table when we walked in. I washed my hands in the bathroom as I took in all the smells of home. As I set down at the table, my curiosity grew. Pointing to a door at the end of the hall I asked, "What do you keep in there?"

"Nothing. When we moved in it looked like everything was placed in there for a reason, and since we didn't need the extra room, we just left it."

"Excuse me," I said, getting up from the table and going over to the room at the end of the hall.

"What are you doing? Dad just said that it's supposed to be left alone!" Alison's little brother, Alex, said.

Ignoring him, I took a hold of the doorknob and turned it. It opened freely, and I stood in the doorway.

"This was Jerry's room. My dad and I always let it be just the way Jerry had left it. It looks just the same as the day he went away."

The man was standing behind me. "Kiddo, it's about time you told us who you are."

He was right. I couldn't beat around the bush any

longer, so I went back to the table, sat down, and told them who I really was. After I'd told them about my dad being called up and running away from the Johnsons the man spoke up.

"Well, Lillian, my name's Mr. Robinson. This is my son Alex and my daughter Alison. I'll make you a deal. You can stay with us as long as you want, and when you think it's time to move on, you can take your horse Buttercup and go. What do you say?"

"Sounds good. I'll stay in Jerry's room so Alison doesn't have to move out."

The rest of supper, I talked to the Robinsons about things, and afterward we played a boardgame. When it was time for bed, I got ready, said good night, and then slipped into Jerry's bed. As I snuggled into the covers and the pillow, I breathed in the smell of the brother I'd loved so much. As I was drifting off to sleep, I knew one thing for sure. I was, at last, home.

CHAPTER 12

I woke up to the familiar smells of home. The sun was just cresting in the east, so I slid out of bed, put on my jeans and a t-shirt, then opened up one of the dresser drawers and slipped on one of Jerry's old button-downs. The arms were too long, so I rolled them up so that my hands could move freely. After I'd grabbed my bridle out of my backpack, I noiselessly made my way toward the front door. After I was out of the house and I had my riding boots on, I headed for the corral. This time when I whistled for Buttercup she came. I greeted her with a piece of carrot. "How'd you like to go for a sunrise ride just like we use to?"

She tossed her head in response, so I took it to be a yes. I gave her a quick brush down, then slipped on the leather bridle. I'd just woven the bit into it the day before, and it fit her like a glove. I led her through the gate, then, using the fence as a mounting block, I mounted her bare back. After I got her warmed up a bit, I took a secure grip on her mane, and we rode like the wind. I pulled her to a stop under a big live oak tree, laid my head down, and hugged her neck, just like old times. I hadn't realized how much time had gone by when I looked at the sun and it was full up. I figured I'd best head back to the house before they started wondering where I'd headed off to.

When I got back to the house, I gave Buttercup a good rub down and let her into the pasture. Everyone was already sitting down at the table for breakfast when I came in.

"Good morning. Sorry I'm late, I went for a sunrise ride on Buttercup."

Before anyone else could say a word, Alison chimed in. "But how could you have? When I went out to the tack room this morning, Buttercup's bridle, saddle, and everything were still there just the way I left it."

"On my morning rides I don't use a saddle, and for a bridle I used the one I made."

"Ride? Without a saddle? How?"

"It's called bareback riding. My dad taught me how to feel the horse beneath you and to hold on with your knees."

Before Alison could ask any more questions, Mr. Robinson put in, "Hold on, you two. You can talk the ins and outs of horse riding *after* breakfast. Right now, eat up while it's hot."

Then, turning to me, he said, "Lillian, I found a package in the closet in the master bedroom. I thought you might like to have it."

He handed it to me and I looked at the postmark. It was from Vietnam. The address was in Jerry's handwriting, and the delivery date was the day the telegram came with the news of his death. With shaking hands, I cut the packing tape to reveal what was inside. The first thing I saw was a folded piece of paper. I opened it and had a rush of sadness when I saw what was written on it.

Dear Dad,

I thought you might like this. One of the women who we

66

delivered rations to made it. Please tell Lillian how much I love her, and that I can't wait to go on a camping trip with her when I get home. Dad, I can't put into words what I've seen and the things I've experienced while serving in Vietnam. Everyday something tests my faith, but with God's help I've been able to stay close to Him even in the midst of trials. Well, I need to go. I love you, Dad.

Love, Jerry.

I folded the letter and took out what was in the box. It was a box woven out of thick grasses. It was beautiful. Whoever made it used different-colored grasses to create designs on the box. My heart hurt as I remembered all that Jerry and I were going to do. I got up from the table and took the box to Jerry's room. I set the letter inside and set the box on Jerry's dresser.

When breakfast was through, I went out to finish grooming Buttercup. I was so lost in imagining what I'd do over the next couple weeks that I hadn't heard Alison walk in.

"You love her, don't you?"

"Yeah, I guess you could say that. We've grown up together. My mom gave her to me the spring before she died. I turned six that fall, right after she died. But she's with God now, so I know she's not sad or hurting."

"Can you teach me how to ride bareback?"

"Are you ready to learn?"

"Sure."

"Okay, let me go get Ginger so we can work together."

I fetched Ginger from the pasture, then we got them ready. We headed out to the pasture, where there weren't any rocks that we'd get hurt on if either one of the horses acted up. We started out slow until I got back into the feel of Ginger. I remembered my first lesson my dad gave me on bareback riding and tried to teach Alison the same. At first, she didn't understand, but once she did, she caught on and looked like she was a natural. All morning we worked together and got a lot done. When noon came, we headed back to the house for lunch.

We rubbed down the horses and gave them fresh water and grain. As we went inside, Mr. Robinson stopped us. "Girls, I need you to do me a favor. One of the fences close to the train track is in ill repair, so could you two go out there and fix it this afternoon? I would do it, but I need to meet my friend in town."

"Sure, Mr. Robinson, we can do out right after we have lunch."

I was eager to get back out working again, but Alison didn't feel quite the same way. "Aw, Dad. Do I have to? Can't you just have Alex do it?"

"No, I asked you to do it."

After we had lunch, I filled a canteen and saddled Buttercup so we could ride out to where the fence was needing repair. In order to know what I'd need to take, I asked Mr. Robinson, "What's wrong with the fence?"

"Some of the barbwire is rusted, to the point if any pressure is put on it at all, it would give way."

"Alright, so I'll restring that section."

I took a coil of barbwire, wrapped it in thick canvas, then tied it to the back of the saddle. Alison had whined enough to get out of it, so I was on my own. Before heading out, I took a pair of thick work gloves and the other tools I'd need to repair the fence. Once I'd reached the place where the fence was damaged, I dismounted then inspected it.

Mr. Robinson was right, it was really rusty at the points where it was attached to the posts, so I needed to restring two sections. The sections were six feet long, so I needed a total of three twelve-foot pieces of wire, with a foot at each end to attach it to the post. The first thing I did was take off the old wire; if I wasn't careful, I could get cut on the wire. The first step went well, and I moved on to stretching out the wire into manageable pieces. This was the hardest step, since if I didn't do it right, the wire could coil back and cut me. I'd done this so many times that I could do it without hurting myself. I worked hard, and even yet if I were to do it too fast, I'd risk hurting myself. I worked slowly and steadily, so by the time I was done the sun told me it was time to head to the house.

When I pulled Buttercup up in front of the house, Alison was waiting for me. "What took you so long?"

"If I did the job any faster, I'd have probably have come back all cut up, and the job still wouldn't be done."

I took care of Buttercup and was washing up when Mr. Robinson got out of his car and came toward me. "Lillian, I just went out to the section of fence that you repaired. It looks as good as new."

"Yes, sir."

"I'll make you a deal. How'd you like to work for me, be sort of a ranch hand? I got a job in town, and there are things around here that my children can't take care of, so I'd need to hire someone anyways. If you work for me and keep up the physical part of the ranch, then I'll pay for everything needed to keep this ranch alive. If you need extra help, then you can act as my foreman and enlist Alex to help you. Along with the pay, you can have free room and board. What do you say?"

69

"One condition. I use Buttercup as my own. I know her and we work well together. If Alison wants to ride, then she can ride Ginger, my Dad's horse."

"It's a deal. I'll put you on the payroll starting tomorrow morning."

It felt good knowing I had a job. How long would I stay there? I didn't know, but I had a job, and I was home.

CHAPTER 13

Over the next few days, the work was hard. I'd get up with the sun and go to bed not long after dinner. One morning I was about to go ride the fence line when in the far distance I saw a funnel cloud. A shiver ran down my back, and I ran to the house.

"Tornado! Everyone! Get in the cellar!"

I yelled as I turned and took off for the barn. I had to release all the animals before the tornado came. I had just let out the chickens when I was almost plumb blown off my feet by the wind. I hunched my back and forced my way to the cellar door. Everybody was in, so when I was fully in I heaved the door shut and latched it. While I'd taken care of the animals, Mrs. Robinson had shut and barred all the shutters on the house. Even inside the cellar I could hear the wind whipping around the house. As we sat and looked at each other, time seemed to crawl. After what felt like hours, the wind had died down and all was silent. Being very cautious, I unlatched the door and peeped my head out to look around, not knowing what to expect. To my relief, the house and barn were still standing. I told the rest of the Robinsons that it was all clear, then I climbed up into the open air.

I had just come out of the barn after checking it over when I saw Mr. Robinson's car coming up the drive.

He hopped out of the car and came toward where I was standing. "Thank God you're alright. What about the rest of the family?"

"They're fine, sir, we hustled into the cellar in time. They're in the house."

"Any significant damage around here?"

"I let the livestock out of the barn before the tornado hit, so now they're scattered all over tarnation. Besides that, a broken window, and some shingles that came off. We were fortunate; the storm missed the barn, corral, and house."

"Well, I'll take care of the livestock. On the way home I saw the fence near the highway. All that's left is a mess of tangled barbed wire and broken fence posts. That'll need to be repaired rather quickly so that the cattle don't get near the highway."

"I'll do that right away, sir. It can't be much latter than mid-morning, so if I get started right away, I'll be able to get a good start on it today."

Turning, I walked back in to the barn and found the large pile of fence posts my dad had made up. I loaded and strapped a bunch of them onto our John Deere Gator, gathered the tools I'd need to set the posts, and went to the house to get the rest of what I'd need. After I'd filled my canteen and put together a bag of lunch, I headed out. As I passed Jerry's room, I snatched my rifle and some ammunition so I could do some coyote hunting if I happened to be out at dusk. I drove the Gator down our driveway till I reached a place where I could cut across toward the highway. I had no idea what to expect when I came into view of the fence line. It was torn up all the way down a long stretch. As a consequence, it was going to take me more than an afternoon. I started at one end where the standing fence remained. The fence posts were taken off at the base. I leaned my rifle against the Gator and started digging up the posts one by one, replacing them with new posts.

I was working so hard trying to get the fence repaired that I didn't notice dark clouds gathering until I felt a big drop of rain plop on the back of my neck. By the time I looked up, the raindrops were coming down like cats and dogs. I put the rest of the materials I hadn't used in the Gator and began driving back in the rain. It made me remember the day Jerry and I got caught in a rainstorm.

I had just turned six, and we were out on the very first overnight ride without Mom or Dad when it started to rain. "Jerry, what are we going to do? It's too far to ride back in the rain!"

As panicked as I was, Jerry kept his calm. "Hold on, little one. There's a cabin Dad and I built not far from here."

We made camp in the cabin, and Jerry started a campfire out of some kindling that he'd kept dry in a wood box. As we watched the flames and listened to the rain pound down on the roof, I thought about Mom. "Jerry, I can't wait for Mom to recover so she can be out here with us."

"Lillian, that's what I need to talk to you about."

His voice wasn't as full as life as it usually was. It made me curious. "What do you mean, 'That's what I need to talk to you about?'"

"She'll never be out here with us again."

Not wanting to understand what I thought he may

have been saying, I asked again, "What do you mean?!"

I almost screamed it. But Jerry kept his voice calm and steady. "Lillian, Mom died last night. Dad wanted me to take you out on this ride so he could have us out of the house while he sorts things out."

I don't remember much of what happened that night. What I do remember is that Jerry took me in his arms and held me for what felt like hours.

From that day on, whenever we'd have a rain storm, I'd be taken back to that night.

When I finally got home, I was soaked to the bone. I drove the Gator into the barn, then headed for the house. I was a sight to be seen when I knocked on that door. Mr. Robinson opened it and immediately wrapped me in towels and ushered me into the laundry room. "Whatever happened to you?"

"Got caught in the downpour. I didn't notice it until it was upon me."

"Well, next time be more aware of your surroundings, and this won't happen."

I slipped into some of Jerry's old, clean clothes. At dinner, Mrs. Robinson handed me a letter. When I slit it open, my dad's dog tags fell out, along with a letter.

Dear Lillian Hartley,

Here are your dad's dog tags. They were found where your dad was last seen. We had a complete search done of the area, and no sign of him was found. That's the end of the story. Now, even if someone could find him, they couldn't identify him, since he doesn't have his dog tags. Even though it's not official, your dad might as well be reported killed in action, since the last gleam of hope has faded. Again, I am truly sorry.

Yours,

Mr. Ash

I clenched my teeth so hard I thought I might break my jaw. I went over to the wood stove, opened the door, then crumpled up the letter and threw it in. When I turned back to the table, Alex was playing with Dad's dog tags. "What are these?"

I walked over, took them from his hand, and without a word went to Jerry's room. After I slipped on Dad's dog tags, I packed a set of Jerry's clothes and a couple other essentials into my saddlebags. I went over to the closet and gathered Jerry's bedroll, an oil burning lantern, and last, but not least, Jerry's old worn leather cowboy hat. I put it all by the foot of my bed so I'd be ready to go first thing in the morning. Next, I went out to the barn. As I walked through the kitchen, no one stopped me. No one even said anything. I just kept my eyes on the door. When I got to the barn, I polished every nook and cranny of my tack. Next, I gave Buttercup a full groom down.

"When are you pulling out?" Mr. Robinson was standing in the barn doorway.

"First thing in the morning."

"I'm not going to try to convince you to stay, but can I at least ask one question?"

"Go right ahead."

"Why? Why are you going now? You've been working for me for weeks and all of a sudden you want to leave?"

"I have no reason to stay. I have nothing to tie me down here anymore."

"In what way?"

"Before that letter came, I had hope. There was

just a sliver of a chance that my dad might be found and come home. But now that his dog tags were found and he wasn't, that sliver is gone."

"Well, I can't say I'm not going to miss you. You're the hardest working girl I've ever known, and if you ever need a job you've always got one here."

"Thank you, sir."

With that he turned and walked into the house. I finished getting Buttercup ready, then headed in myself. As I lay one last night in Jerry's bed, I thought about everything that had happened in this house and all the memories that went with it. Before long, though, I was sound asleep.

CHAPTER 14

I woke up before dawn, picked up my belongings, and went out to the kitchen. It was still dark out and no one was awake yet, so I wrote a note on a notepad, set it on the table, and took one last look around the last place I had to call home. I headed out to the barn and saddled up Buttercup, including the big pair of saddlebags, rifle and rifle saddle, and Jerry's bed roll. When I rode out into the fresh morning air, the sun was just throwing its first gleams into the eastern sky. The air was brisk and I was ready to ride.

First thing was first. I was going to have a day to myself. I wasn't going to take the main trail that we usually took when we used to go to the far section of the property. Instead, I cut up across over the hills. At one part it took fancy footwork on the horse's part, but if you were a good horseman with a loyal horse it was a breeze, and it was also shorter than the main trail.

Then I came to the top of a hill. It was the highest one around, so I could see for miles. The morning air was clear and sweet as I gazed out over the land and took it all in. To the east was our ranch house and barn, and to the west lay miles and miles of rolling hills. Winding down through the gorge in the hills was our river. At a bend in the river sat our cabin, where I'd spent many a night with my dad and Jerry. The river served as the far border of our property. Scattered over it all was our cattle. Some were grazing and some were drinking from the streams that led to the river. All of it, the hills, the river, the endless blue sky in every direction, was what made our ranch home.

After resting Buttercup for a minute, I continued toward the river. However, we didn't stop there. We turned upstream till we came to a place where there was a small inlet that made a deep clear pool where there was hardly any current. Beside the pool, there was a big oak tree and a bolder. I dismounted, took the saddlebags, saddle, and bedroll off Buttercup, then did something I had wanted to do since the day we had received the telegram.

After I wiped Buttercup down, I mounted her bareback, took hold of the reins, and we were off, galloping over the rolling hills. I was free, free from everything, free from school, free from the city life, with the wind whipping at my face and feeling the ground pound beneath me as I rode; at last, I was free as an eagle. When Buttercup and I were both worn out, we rode back to where we had made camp.

I took the bridle off of Buttercup, wiped her down, then ground tied her where she had plenty of fresh grass. On one side of the swimming hole, I set a fishing line with a few baited hooks on it to catch some dinner. It was a warm fall day, so I changed into my swimsuit, climbed to the top of the boulder, then *ploosh*. I dived in deep, then started to swim directly toward the surface. The chill of the water went straight to my bones, but it felt so good. I swam to the shore, then, after resting a second, I climbed out and jumped in again. This time I took a big enough of a breath that while I was underwater, I could open up my eyes and look around.

After I swam till I felt too tired to swim any more, I climbed out and lay on the boulder to let the sun dry me. After I was dry, I got dressed, started a campfire, then went to check my fishing line. I had caught a good size rainbow trout. By the time I gutted it, my fire was ready to cook on. I took a little bag out of my saddlebag that had some pepper and a couple other herbs in it, rubbed it into the fish, and cooked it over the fire. It was delicious. After I'd washed my tin plate, fork and knife, and cup, I put them away in my saddlebags. I climbed up on the boulder to watch the sun set. Once it had dipped under the horizon, I got off the boulder. In the last gleams of dusk, I went over, brought Buttercup, and tethered her by the oak tree, then rolled out my bedroll by the warmth of the fire, got my blanket, and laid down by the fire to sleep.

CHAPTER 15

Over the next few days, I got to know the land of Texas outside our area. I rode for hours at a time to get from one town to the next. I lived under the stars by night and under the beating sun by day. In the small towns and at ranch houses along the way, I found odd jobs which kept enough food in the pot to keep me going. Soon, though, I realized that I'd need to find a steady job so one day I could continue to raise the best beef in all of Texas. In every small town I went into, I picked up a newspaper and scanned it for ranch hand ads, and my eyes tended to look for an article about an unknown soldier found. I finally found an ad for a ranch hand. I rode up to the place and dismounted. I knocked on the door and showed him the ad. "Good morning, sir. I've come in response to this ad in the paper for a ranch hand."

"I'm sorry, but we don't hire on children here. Especially not girls. Goodbye."

And at that he shut the door on me. I turned, mounted Buttercup, and rode off. I rode into the small town, tied Buttercup behind one of the stores, and went in to replenish supplies. I went in the store, and after I'd gathered my supplies, I went to the front counter to pay. I saw another ranch hand ad. I still had enough daylight and it wasn't far off, so I decided to find the ranch and ask about the job before I made camp for the night. I approached the house and asked for the name in the ad. Again, it was the same story, no girls. I was riding away disheartened when the man called, "Hey kid! Wait up. I said I didn't need another ranch hand; I didn't say I don't need someone to work around the house. Can you chop wood?"

"Yes, sir."

"Clean the stables?"

"Yes, sir."

"Then you've got the job. Room and board in the hayloft and you get paid every two weeks."

"It's a deal."

I took Buttercup to the stables and made sure she had fresh water and oats, then I put my tack in the hayloft. Over the next couple days, I learned the ways of the ranch. I was just a stable hand, yet that meant when the men came in from riding, I got to take care of the horses. I was getting paid to do what I loved. The only thing that could make it better was for me to be out on the open range.

One day, I went into the house and saw a flyer for a rodeo. Starting that day, as soon as I got my work done around the place, I'd go over to the large corral, set up the barrels, and practice with Buttercup for hours. I hadn't done much when I was little, but I'd done enough for me to know a thing or two about it. Rain or shine, I'd be out there nearly every day riding. One day I looked up and saw that one of the other hands was watching me.

"That's not bad."

"I plan to compete at the upcoming rodeo."

"I wouldn't advise it."

"Why?"

"You haven't got the horse for that. I've been watching you and your horse is strong, but she hasn't got what it takes for a barrel riding. If you do compete with her, you could risk laming her."

"Alright, thanks for the advice. I think I'll take it."

I stopped training her for barrel racing. Instead, I readied her to leave the ranch. I'd been there for a few weeks and it was time to move on. Soon I was ready to go. I gave them word that I was leaving, and they gave me my final pay.

I was on my own once again. Then it began to rain and the wind began to blow. The rain came in big drops rolling down my jacket and off Buttercup. Pretty soon I was drenched. I looked around at the landscape and it seemed dulled by the rain. After I rode for a long time, I came upon a stand of pines. One was an old pine tree with the bows reaching all the way to the ground. Therefore, it made a sort of tepee. I walked around it till I found a small opening where the pine boughs parted a bit. I cautiously stepped into the darkness. It was damp, but it was a little warmer, and sheltered from the wind and rain. I unsaddled Buttercup, put the things just inside the opening, and then took the tether line from my saddlebag, attaching one end to Buttercup's halter and the other end to a branch just inside the doorway. In the dark dampness I took some jerky from my saddlebag and chewed on it while I thought. By now it must have been at least a couple of months since I'd left the Johnsons. As I went over in my mind what had happened since I'd left, I laughed. I'd had good times and bad, and now I was going to find a new start. Somewhere where they wouldn't care if I was a girl or if I had a family. Starting now, I had a clean slate. Everything else was behind me and I was ready for a fresh start.

CHAPTER 16

I needed to pick up some supplies, so I left Buttercup at a farm outside a big city, then ventured in on foot. Once I was in the suburbs, I caught a bus that would take me to the city center. When I got off the bus I heard a commotion in the city square, so I decided to go check it out. As I got closer, I could see people waving signs with things like "Make peace, not war!" and "Nixon, get out of Vietnam!" written on them. It was one of the antiwar peace rallies that my dad had told me about. I was wearing one of Jerry's ROTC shirts that he got when he still wanted to go to college instead of just enlisting. Well, when they saw my shirt and dog tags, I became a target. Before I knew it, people were screaming at me. One person even picked up a rock and chucked at me. It missed, but I knew I had to get out before the rally became a riot. Too late; I tried to push my way through the crowd, but the people kept pushing me around. I held tight onto my bag and kept trying. Just as I thought I was trapped, a man grabbed my arm and shouted, "Come on! We gotta get out of here!"

He began pulling me though the crowd as people yelled at us, calling us things so bad I'd never heard them before. People continued to chuck rocks at us as the man who was still holding onto me pulled me though the crowd. I probably would have tried to twist free if I hadn't been so relieved about getting out of that mess. I felt something hit the side of my head, and my vision fogged up for just a second.

After what felt like ages of pushing and shoving though the crowd, we were at last out in the open. He didn't stop though; he kept running, pulling me behind him until we'd crossed the street and had run two blocks away from the rally. Only then did he slow us down to a walk. I was gasping for breath by then, and my hand was pure white from gripping my bag so hard. He stopped us out in front of an ice cream parlor and tried to catch his breath. I dropped my bag and worked my hand open and shut to get some blood back into it. Then I felt something running down the side of my head. My hand shot up and I could feel where the rock that hit me had torn a gash into the side of my head. The blood had run down the side of my head and dried. Once the man had caught his breath, he straightened up and said, "Well I'm sorry about that, I didn't mean to push you so hard."

"That's okay, you got us out alive, didn't you?"

"Yeah, I guess I did. I should introduce myself. I'm Jason, Jason Thomas. What's your name?"

"Lillian, Lillian Hartley. Mr. Thomas, you don't sound like you're from Texas."

"Well, I'm actually not, and just call me Jason. I'm here as a student. I'm a ROTC cadet at University of Texas. When I saw you with your dog tags and ROTC shirt, I knew you'd be a target. By the way, what was a kid like you doing at a riot like that?"

"It was an accident. I'd come into town to get supplies and found myself smack dab in the center of the riot."

That was when he noticed the blood on the side of my head. "Come on, let's go into this ice cream parlor here and get that gash fixed up."

We went in and took a seat at the counter. Jason called to one of the guys working there. "Hey, Joe, bring me some wet paper towels and some antiseptic if you've got any."

"Jason, why would you want any antiseptic? What happened? Have another run in with those hippies?"

"No, it's not for me, it's for a kid I'm with. Just bring it, won't ya?"

"Okay, okay. I'm coming, I'm coming."

A man came out from the back room with some wet paper towels and a bottle of antiseptic.

"Here you go. Whoa. Who's the girl?"

"The kid I was telling you about. She was stuck in the antiwar protest and so I got her out. On our way through the crowd, though, she got hit on the side of the head."

Jason took the paper towels and used them to wipe the blood off the side of my head. Then, taking a fresh paper towel, he wet it with antiseptic and said, "This is going to hurt some."

He wiped the wound, and boy! That did hurt. By then his friend Joe had come back with some bandages and medical tape to tape them on with. After he'd cleaned the wound, Jason put a bandage on it, then taped it on so it wouldn't go anywhere.

"There," he said, "that should last a while. Now, how 'bout a soda?"

"Sure."

"Cola sound alright?"

"Yup."

"Joe, bring us a couple of Colas."

"Coming right up." he called.

While Joe got us our sodas, Jason turned to me and said, "So, Lillian, what are you doing with an ROTC shirt?"

"Well, my brother was going to do ROTC in college."

"Was?"

"Yeah. Then the government began calling for more troops, so he enlisted and said he was going to do college when he got back."

"Well did he? I mean, did he do college when his time was up?"

"Nope. He didn't make it back. He was killed at the Battle of La Drang."

By then Joe had brought us our sodas, and we drank them in silence. After a while I looked up at the clock and realized that if I wanted to make camp by nightfall, I'd better get my supplies and go fetch Buttercup. I thanked Jason for the soda, then asked him where the closest grocery store was. He said, "Three blocks down the street on the left, away from the riot."

"Thanks, see ya."

I walked out of the soda fountain and headed down the street away from the riot. At the grocery store I bought the food I needed, then, when I was a couple blocks away, I went back and got some bandages so I could keep the cut on the side of my head clean. I walked to the bus route and waited for a bus to take me out of town.

It was dark by the time I got back to the ranch where I left Buttercup. I paid the family for the use of one of their stalls and headed into the setting sun to find a place to make camp. It was full dark and the stars were coming out by the time I'd made a campfire and got some meat roasting. I spent the night under the stars and come morning I headed out in search of a job.

CHAPTER 17

The days blended together as I lived under the stars and searched, with no success, for a job. One day I was following a small road in the middle of nowhere when Buttercup became skittish. I tried to calm her down, yet she kept getting worse, until all of a sudden, she threw me. It wouldn't have been that bad, except that my right ankle was caught in the stirrup. I got flung up, then lurched to the ground. Thankfully, when I lurched to the ground, my ankle released from the stirrup and came to the ground with me. When I hit the ground, I felt a sharp pain in my head and saw stars. I don't know how long I was unconscious; it must have been a while, since when I came to there was a man with a wet cloth blotting my forehead.

With one hand I tried to push him away when he spoke to me in a soft, kind voice, "It's alright, child, I won't hurt you."

"Wha… what happened?" I was trying to focus on the man's face.

"Your horse showed up at my corral. I followed its tracks and came to a little girl who looked like she was thrown."

"Thanks. If you hadn't come along, I'd be a goner."

"You still might be if your dad sees you like that.

Just tell me where you live. I'll make sure you get home safely, then explain to your father what happened."

I winced as I tried get up. "No, that won't be necessary, I can tell him what happened."

"You can tell him, sure, if you even get home. Girl, you are worse off than you think. You have at least a sprained--maybe broken--ankle, a gash on your head, and who knows what else."

"But..."

"No buts about it. I'm going to get you home if it kills me. Well?"

I bit my lip to keep me from crying. "I don't have a father, a home, or anything."

"Then where do you live?"

I pointed up at the sky. "Under that."

"On your own."

"Yup, just like I have been for the past few months."

"What about your dad?"

"He was a Marine reserve in active duty, and when he went missing in action, I ran away from the family I'd been staying with to live under the stars."

"Well, you're in no shape to sleep under the stars tonight, so you're coming home with me."

He slowly eased his arms under me and picked me up. He helped me on to Buttercup. "You think you can hold yourself up there at least for a little ways?"

"Yes, sir."

I touched my head with my hand, and I could feel that he had tied a strip of cloth around the cut on my head. The ride was long, and it seemed like we were in the middle of nowhere. When at last we came to a small farmhouse, a woman came out to meet us.

"Steven, what in the world did you bring me this time?"

The next thing I noticed were a couple of kids standing by the barn door. He led me to the corral, tied Buttercup to one of the rails, and helped me down.

"Honey, I found this girl whose horse bucked her a couple miles off."

Then he turned to me. "What's your name?"

"Lillian, sir."

"Then, Lillian, let's get you inside and clean you up."

He helped me inside and sat me down in a kitchen chair.

He explained to his wife what happened, and pretty soon they'd taken off the bandage on my head and cleaned my cut and rebandaged it. Once they'd fixed up my head, they started on my ankle. They carefully slipped off my riding boot and sock. My ankle had swollen, and it was a little black and blue. They immediately laid a bag of ice wrapped in a towel on my ankle. After they'd iced it for a while, Mrs. Phillips kneeled and worked her hands up and down my ankle, feeling every inch of it.

When she stood up, she said, "Can you move your toes, Lillian?"

With all my might I tried to wiggle my toes, and they wouldn't move. The only thing I felt was pain coming from my leg. "No, ma'am, I can't."

She turned to her husband, saying, "Steven, her ankle is either fractured or broken, so you'd better make her a splint."

He walked out of the room and a girl came in. She

looked to be about my age, with red hair and freckles. Her mom introduced me to her.

"Lillian, this is Becky. Becky, this is Lillian."

"Hi, how long are you staying with us?"

In response, I looked at Mrs. Phillips. "Until she's all healed," she said.

"Well, being it looks like you'll be here a while, do you want me to bring down a pack of cards so we can play at the table?"

"Alright," I replied with a smile.

Before long we had a lively game of cards going. We were playing the kinds of games we used to play at home once our homework was done. After a while Becky had snagged her brother, and once Mr. Phillips had put the splint on my leg, he played too. As the hours rolled by we joked and laughed together. We only stopped when Mrs. Phillips put the roast beef down on the center of the table. Supper was delicious, from the roast beef to the baked potatoes.

When the supper dishes were cleared, Mr. Phillips gave me the crutch he'd made me and showed me how to use it to move from the kitchen to the family room. Once settled in the family room, Mr. Phillips read to us from *Robinson Crusoe*. After he'd read a couple of chapters, he picked up the family Bible, opened it, and began reading.

"'Whom shall I send, and who will go for Us?' Then I said, 'Here am I! Send me.'"

As I listened to the rest of Isaiah chapter six, I looked around the room. I saw this family and felt something warm inside me. Once Mr. Phillips had finished reading, I took my crutch and hobbled out to the front doorway. I stood looking up at the stars, thinking about what had happened.

"They're beautiful, aren't they, Lillian?"

"Yes, sir. I was just thinking about how tonight, for the first time since my dad was called up to be sent to Vietnam, I felt like I really belong."

We stood watching the stars for a long time together. When it came time, I shared a room with Becky. The last thing I saw before I drifted off to sleep was the light coming from Mr. and Mrs. Phillips's room.

CHAPTER 18

The first thing I smelled as I awoke was fresh coffee. Voices wafted up the stairs as I looked over and saw Becky still in bed. My saddlebags were at the foot of my bed, so I reached down and took out a set of fresh clothes. Using my crutches, I went down the hall to the bathroom and changed. As I came down the stairs and into the kitchen, Mr. Phillips said, "Good morning, Lillian, want some coffee?"

"Good morning. No, thank you."

My dad wouldn't let us drink coffee until our eighteenth birthday. That was the rule in our house, and we stuck to it.

Mrs. Phillips turned from where she was making breakfast. "Come over here, Lillian, and we'll clean and apply a clean bandage on that wound of yours."

I flinched as she carefully peeled the bandage off the wound.

"How does it look, Caroline?"

"Well, it's not infected or swollen, and it's starting to heal at the edges."

I asked a question I'd been wondering since I'd been bucked. "How long till I can ride?"

"Well, it's not the head that determines that as much as the ankle. Speaking of which, let's check it out."

93

She propped my leg up on a chair, taking care she started to remove the pieces of splint. That hurt more than my head.

"By the looks of it, you'll need to stay off of it for a couple more days, maybe even a couple weeks."

"Yes, ma'am." My hopes deflated. A couple weeks? How could I stay in one place without riding for a couple weeks?

Mrs. Phillips fixed up both my head and my ankle. Becky came in the kitchen and greeted us cheerfully.

"Lillian, do you want to make friendship bracelets with me after breakfast?"

"Sure."

For breakfast we had eggs and bacon, after which we cleared the table and Becky laid out various colors of string. We sat at the table for hours making one bracelet after another. After a while I asked her if she had any rawhide. She disappeared into the storeroom and returned with several strips of rawhide. After I'd tied few of them together, I began to weave. Becky took some strips, tied them together, and then tried to copy what I was doing. I could tell she wasn't having much luck, so I put mine down and showed her how to start the weave. It was fun to teach her what Jerry had taught me so long ago. Once she got the hang of it, I showed her how you could weave in different colored ribbons.

Remembering the bridle, I'd made for Buttercup, I went upstairs and fetched it from my saddlebags.

"It's beautiful," Becky said as she ran her hands over it.

"It took me months to make. If I did a single weave that I didn't like, I took it out and redid it."

"Can you teach me to weave like this?"

"I can sure try."

I taught her everything that Jerry had taught me, step by step until I had taught her every weave I knew. Late afternoon rolled around and Mr. Phillips and Jacob came in from working. After they washed up, we sat around the table playing cards. They taught me a couple new games and I taught them one or two that I knew and they didn't.

When it was almost time for dinner, Jacob came in, hiding something in his jacket. He came over to me. "Lillian, put out your arms and close your eyes. I have a surprise for you."

I did so, having no idea what to expect. I smiled ear to ear when I felt a soft warm ball placed in my hands. I opened my eyes and looked right at a little puppy. It was brown and looking up at the wide world.

"It's so cute."

"Yeah, well, our lab had a litter in the barn, so I thought you might like to have him so he could keep you company."

Becky was delighted by the surprise and asked, "Well, what are you going to name him?"

I thought for a minute, looking at this little brown Labrador retriever pup sitting in my arms. The first thing that came to mind was an old friend of mine. "His name will be Jerry."

"Why Jerry?"

"Because he was the most faithful brother I ever had."

Jacob said he would help me house train the pup, but for now he had to go back out to the barn for dinner. After dinner, Mr. Phillips read aloud from *Robinson Crusoe* then the bible. Part of me wished I could stay there for the rest of my life, but deep down I knew that I had head out and find work as soon as I was healed.

CHAPTER 19

From then on, I stayed with the Phillips'. Every waking moment I spent training Jerry. Once my head was healed, I took him on short walks around the farm. He learned quickly, and pretty soon he didn't even need a leash--my voice was his command. I taught him to follow me, and when I stopped, he'd stop. After a few days I introduced him to Buttercup. At first, she was skittish around Jerry, but after a little while they became best of friends. As the days rolled by and I was able to put more pressure on my ankle, I knew the time was coming when I'd have to leave the family, I'd grown so fond of. One morning I came down to breakfast and a surprise awaited me.

Mrs. Phillips greeted me. "Come on over here, Lillian, and let's check your ankle."

She felt it all over to make sure there wasn't any swelling. "Feels all good. I'll tell you what. Why don't you walk from here over to the counter without your crutches?"

It would have been the first time I'd walked without crutches in almost three weeks. I decided to take a chance, so standing up, I slowly took one step then the next. My leg felt stiff, but it didn't hurt or give out.

"Well, how does it feel?"

"It's stiff… but it doesn't hurt."

"Then that splint can come right off."

It felt wonderful as she took the splint off piece by piece. The first thing I did when it was at last off was roll my ankle.

"If you wanted to, darling, you could start ridding today."

The first thing I felt was a burst of joy. I could walk, I could ride! I could be free now, back out on the open range just like I used to be. The next thing I felt was a prickle of pain. Knowing that now I could ride, I'd be leaving the Phillips. I knew this day would come yet, I had grown so close to them that I didn't want to leave.

My thoughts were interrupted by Mr. Phillips coming into the room. "Hey, look at that. Your splint is off. Now you can ride."

"Mr. Phillips, I don't like to be a freeloader. I can pay you for the time I've spent with your family."

A smile started to spread across his face. "I've got a better idea. I need some help on the farm. You've stayed here for almost three weeks, so if you work for me for a week, we can call it fair. What do you say?"

He put out his hand to shake and I did. "It's a deal."

For the first time in a week I got to ride Buttercup. After a full ride, I began to work with Mr. Phillips. We started with repairing the roof of the barn. After a while he asked, "So, how did you learn to work so hard?"

"My father. After my brother enlisted in the Marines, I took on his responsibilities on the ranch."

"Was your ranch large?"

"Yes, sir. We raised open range beef cattle for supermarkets and grocery stores in our area. Our beef was well known throughout some parts of Texas."

"You want to raise beef one day?"

"Yes, sir. Someday I'm going to raise the best beef in all of Texas."

"How?"

"Find a job on a big ranch somewhere. After I earn some money I can start out on my own."

"You belong on a working ranch, not here on a small farm. I'll tell you what. Once we finish the barn roof, I want you to pack your saddlebags and go."

"But you said…"

"I know what I said. However, if you help me finish this job, that will be enough and we'll call it square."

"Alright, yet why?"

"Because I can tell you don't belong on a small farm in the middle of nowhere. You belong out on the open range working cattle, or helping break in horses. Now, let's get down to it so we can be done by dinner."

"Yes, sir."

We worked for the entire afternoon until we got the job done. At dinner, Mr. Phillips said that I had an announcement to make. All eyes turned to me. At first, I didn't know what he was talking, about then I remembered our conversation from earlier that day. "What Mr. Phillips means is that I'm leaving tomorrow morning. Now that my ankle is healed, I'm able to go find a job to work at and earn some money."

Jacob asked, "Where will you work?"

"On a big ranch somewhere, probably."

For the rest of dinner, we talked, joked, and

99

laughed. As soon as I was through eating, I slipped up to the room I was sharing with Becky and began to pack my saddlebags.

I was just folding my clean set of clothes when Becky came. "You know, I'm really going to miss you out here. Because of where we live, I hardly ever have another girl around to keep me company."

"I can imagine."

"Well, at least you'll have Jerry to remind you of us."

"Becky, I've been thinking about that."

"And?"

"Buttercup and I will be traveling fast, and many miles. I don't think Jerry could keep up with us since he's still just a pup. That and I don't know if I'd be able to feed him while I'm under the stars. Why don't you keep him so you remember me?"

"Sure."

I finished packing my saddlebags, then went downstairs for the family reading. Before long, it was time for bed.

CHAPTER 20

I woke up long before dawn, while the farm was still asleep. Trying not to wake up Becky, I gathered my things and tiptoed down the stairs. There was a plate of breakfast and a sack lunch sitting on table with a note. I ate breakfast and put the lunch in my saddlebag. I walked out to the barn and saddled Buttercup. It felt so good to be out in the morning air and walking without a crutch. My first stop would be a small town to replenish my supplies. As I began to ride away, I looked back and saw a light come on in the house. I was riding under the stars for a while before the sun threw its first gleams into the sky. I had left my pup with Jacob and Becky so it could have a fun, full life. After a couple hours of riding, I rode into a small town. After tying Buttercup behind the grocery store, I purchased enough food to last a couple of days. At the checkout there was a newspaper for sale. One thing caught my eye on the front page:

Wanted: Experienced ranch hand.
Pay will be discussed.
Room and board provided.

There was an address listed. Before I left, I asked the clerk, "Sir, do you know how to get to this address?"

"Well, sure. That's the Tait spread, largest ranch in all of this area. Just follow Main Street out of town a few miles and you'll come to a turnoff. Follow that road till you see the ranch house."

"Thank you."

I went out back, stowed my supplies in my saddlebags, and headed on my way. I followed Main Street all the way out of town. For miles there was no sign of human civilization except a strip of asphalt in either direction. After what felt like hours, I saw the turnoff. There was a sign over the turnoff that said Tait Cattle Ranch. I turned off, following the road. As I rode up, I saw the ranch house and bunkhouse with other small buildings. I rode up to the ranch house and tied Buttercup to the hitching rail, then approached the front door.

When I knocked, a tall, well-built man opened the door. "Yes, how may I help you?"

"Hello sir, I'm here about this ad in the newspaper for a ranch hand. It said to come here." I held out the newspaper.

"Yes, that's my ad, but I was looking for someone more…"

"I know you were looking for a man, but I know all the ins and outs of ranch life and I can work as hard as any man."

"No thanks. It's not that I don't believe you, I just don't hire girls."

Defeated, I walked out and swung up into my saddle. I was just riding away when he called out, "Hey kid, I want to see you ride, then I'll decide if I can give you a try."

"Yes, sir."

He pointed out a tree far off, then a small watering hole a little ways from it. He told me to circle around the tree, then around the watering hole and straight back to him. I got Buttercup lined up, and on his say-so, I took off. I lay myself down till I could just see between her ears. When I reached the tree, I pulled a tight turn and headed for the watering hole. I had to circle wide around it because of its size, but on the straight away I made up the time, and for the finale I pulled Buttercup to an immediate stop right at his side.

"Well, sir, how'd I do?"

"Better than any man on my spread. You're hired. Come inside and I'll take down your information."

"Yes sir, but if you don't mind, I would like to take care of my horse first."

"I hoped you'd say that. After you unsaddle her you can put her in the corral, then follow me inside."

"Will do."

I took care of Buttercup, I followed him. We went into his office, where he took a seat behind his desk, opened up a book, and took out a fresh pen. He looked up and said, "First things first, what's your name?"

"Lillian Hartley, sir."

"Lillian, is that Scottish?"

"Yes sir, my grandparents came from Scotland right before my father was born--but me? I've got Scottish blood in me, but I'm a pure American."

"That's what I like to hear in a good ranch hand. Age?"

"Almost fifteen, sir."

"Any family in the states?"

"No sir, not that I know of."

"No family? No mother, father, brothers or sisters?"

"Not that are alive, sir. My mother was taken by influenza when I was young, my brother was killed in action, and my father went missing in action just recently."

"I'm sorry to hear that."

"So am I, sir."

"Well, that's all I need from you. There's an empty bunk in the bunkhouse. A man who you might call my foreman comes back tomorrow, and he'll teach you the ropes of my spread. Got it?"

"Yes, sir."

"Good night."

CHAPTER 21

I walked out, got my gear from where I staged it, and headed over to the bunkhouse where Mr. Tait said I there was an empty bunk waiting. As I entered, all eyes turned. I saw looks of shock, bewilderment, and surprise from the men sitting on and around the bunks.

Then one man spoke up. "Who are you, and what are you doing here?"

"I'm the new ranch hand Mr. Tait hired on."

"Okay, you can put your father's stuff on that bunk over there, then get out."

"You don't understand, I *am* the new ranch hand."

"The name on the saddle said Hartley, but you're a *girl!*"

"That's right, my name's Hartley, Lillian Hartley."

Seeing his sneer, I walked over to the empty bunk and tossed my gear on the end. Just as I was about to lay my rifle down it was grabbed from my hands. I spun around and was face-to-face with the man who gave me a hard time when I first came in. "Now, what's a little lady like you doing with a rifle?"

Clenching my teeth, I answered as calmly as I could. "I'd like my rifle back, please."

"No, not before you answer my question."

"I use it for hunting, and when I'm on my own I use it for protection."

"Yeah? And what do you hunt? Rabbits?"

I felt anger bubbling inside me and in my voice. "No, coyotes."

Knowing I would probably start a fight if I stayed there any longer, I took my journal and grabbed my rifle out of his hands, then pushed by him and out of the bunkhouse. Outside once again, I went over and propped my back up against the post of the hitching rail, then opened my journal and began to write.

Dear Journal,

Why me? Why is this happening to me? It's evening now. The bunkhouse is buzzing, but everything else on the ranch is quiet. I'm sitting with my back against one of the hitching rails, watching the sun go down. I've finally got a job, but no one will take me for what I am. In the view of the other ranch hands, all they see is that I'm a girl. There's one ranch hand that is supposed to be coming back from a ride tomorrow; if he's as bad as the rest, I'm leaving. I can do the work just as well as any man, and with Buttercup under me I can ride better than any one of them, though the only one that can see that is the owner of the ranch himself.

"Isn't it a bit late for a pretty little lady to be out by herself?"

His voice startled me; I looked up and saw a man in the last gleams of sunlight sitting on a horse. Then his voice registered.

"Tyler! It's you! Why didn't you tell me you worked here?"

At that he dismounted. "Well sorry, I didn't know you worked here, either. I just got back from checking the border of the spread."

"I just got the job this evening."

"Well I'll be. If I'd known you were going to work for Mr. Tait, I'd have put in a good word for you."

"Thanks, but I got the job just fine without you."

"You got the job? But you're just a…"

"Don't say it!" I interrupted. "I've been told that every single place I go, including here. The only reason I even got the job is because Mr. Tait saw that I can ride and work on the ranch just as good as any other man, even though I'm not one."

I got up, journal in one hand, and leaned my elbows on the hitching rail with my back to Tyler. "If you say that I'm no good just because I'm a girl, then you're just like the rest of them--not even giving me a chance to prove myself."

"Alright, I won't say it, but one thing's for sure: you got spunk."

"I've had to over the past few months."

"I get it. I'll keep your back till the men learn to trust you."

"If you're anything like the Tyler I got to know on the road, then you'll keep your word."

He walked up and leaned on the hitching rail beside me. "That's for sure. What are you thinking about?"

"All the people I thought I could trust. One by one they left my life, until it felt like as soon as I thought I could put my full trust in them, they went away."

"Don't worry," he said, taking his hat and plopping it on my head. "You can trust me, and I'll watch your back. If you want to have any energy tomorrow, you'd better get some sleep."

"Yes, sir. Good night."

I turned to walk away, but before I could get far, he put a hand on my shoulder. "And Lillian, cheer up. I'll be your friend."

CHAPTER 22

The sun was just coming up as I approached the bunkhouse. The door was open, and I could see the men playing poker. I'd been up before dawn for a walk in the brisk air. Their voices rang with laughter. That part didn't surprise me, since I'd gotten used to it by now. What threw me off was what they were talking about. "My brother was drafted to go to 'Nam and what did he do? Escaped to Canada. I think the men who answered the draft notice are cowards--not willing to stand up to the fascist government."

"I heard of some men who didn't even wait to be drafted, but just enlisted."

"I don't see why anyone would leave this life to join up and go to 'Nam."

"I think they just go over to act like a hero--for what? Just to get a medal from the president."

"What's gotten into the leaders, letting young men go free with rifles in Asia?"

"Yeah, they're just killers! I don't get that the government doesn't court-martial the whole lot of them and throw them in prison. They're nothing but murderers!"

I had two options. I could either storm out like a little kid, or calmly walk in and act like it wasn't hurting me as deeply as it was. I decided to take the second approach and act like I hadn't heard the talk about Vietnam. I walked in, poured one of the buckets of water into the wash basin, and set the other beside it.

One of the rougher men noticed me and said, "Kid, what do you think about the men who went to Vietnam?"

"You don't care what I think," I spat back at them.

"No really, I care what you think, but I bet you agree with me that they're all murderers."

"Creg, you're just a fool asking a little girl's opinion on such a manly topic as war," one of the other men called from where he was laying on his bunk.

That was it. I'd had enough of them; I'd show them that I could stand up for what I believed and do it well.

"Actually, I think that the men and women who went to fight in Vietnam were heroes and nothing else. Sure, there might have been one or two rotten ones among them, but the true cowards were the men who ran away from the draft instead of doing their duty and reporting for action. Where would our country be if all the men who served in World War II had run away instead of storming the beaches of Normandy on D-Day? It's because of the men and women who stepped up and answered the call that America remains free. So yeah, there might be a few duds in the bunch, but have a little respect for those who risk their lives so that you can remain free."

My voice was steady as I spoke; I knew that if I got mad, they would make fun of me even more. I had my back facing away from the door, so I didn't notice Mr. Tait come in. At first, the men didn't say anything., I didn't want to stick around and be caught in the next verbal crossfire, so I turned and pushed by Mr. Tait on my way out.

I walked out and leaned against the hitching rail. "That was quite a speech you gave in there." Mr. Tait was standing by me with his hat in his hands.

"They needed to be set straight, and it looked like I was the one to do it. "

"Where'd a pretty girl like you learn all that?"

"My dad, mostly; some from Jerry, though."

"Jerry?"

"Yes, Jerry. He was my brother who enlisted in the Marines right out of high school. In his last letter to me, he reminded me of the greatest love: to lay down one's life for his friend."

Before he could respond, a car drove up the drive and stopped by where we were standing. A man got out and a shiver ran down my back. He was in a Marine dress uniform, and he had a slip of paper in his hand. "Mr. Tait?"

"Yes, that's me."

"I've got a telegram for you."

"No, please, no," he said as he took the telegram and opened it. I didn't have to look at it to see what it said. His face hand gone deathly white as his eyes scanned the telegram. Turning to me, he said, "Lillian, please tell the men to brand the cows for the drive and pick out their strings of horses."

"Yes, sir."

"I won't be joining you today, and I probably won't be going on the drive tomorrow. Tell Tyler that he's

111

in charge, and if any of the men don't like it, they'll have to answer to me later."

"Yes, sir."

I turned and walked to the bunkhouse and opened the door. "Mr. Tait said that we're to brand the cattle and pick out our strings for the drive."

"And what gives you the authority to order us around?" One guy called.

"He did. Now, let's get to work. He won't be working with us today, so he said that you're in charge, Tyler."

"Got it, let's go." At least I had Tyler backing me up.

The day was hard, and the men wouldn't get off my back. Come evening, I went to the house to give Mr. Tait an update on what we'd done. It was after dark by the time I'd taken care of Buttercup and cleaned my tack for the drive to come. I went to the side door and knocked softly on the storm door. Mrs. Tait came to the door and let me in. I knocked as much of the dust off my boots as I could, then followed her inside. "I came to mark in the logbook how many cows we branded today."

"Right this way, honey." She led me to Mr. Tait's office where the logbook was sitting on the desk. "You go ahead and mark it yourself, honey. I don't think Dan's up to it right now."

"Yes, ma'am." I opened the logbook to where he'd left off, filled in each slot, and marked the date. As I closed the logbook I said, "I was there when he got the telegram. How bad is it?"

"Killed in action."

"Just like my brother...well, I'd better be going.

Good night, ma'am."

"Good night, Lillian."

CHAPTER 23

It was still dark when my eyes flicked open. The first thing I did was reach my hand down to the foot of my bunk and make sure the rifle and saddlebags were still there. Just to make sure the men didn't play any tricks on me, I took my rifle and headed outside. The morning was brisk and the sun was just barely peeping over the horizon as I walked over to the corral fence. I stood on the fence rail and thought. I laughed as I remembered the first snow I had ever seen.

I was five that winter, and Dad had read to us all about snow in *A Christmas Carol.* Jerry had seen snow before, but I was only one, so I didn't remember it. It was early morning when Jerry started nudging me to wake me up and whispered, "Eaglet, wake up cutie, we don't want to wake up Dad, so you had better get dressed quietly and come with me."

I rolled over in my bed and saw him looking at me with a grin. "Why do I need to get up? Did something happen?"

"Just look out the window."

His voice had something mysterious in it. I got up and walked to the window, then nearly squealed and said in a whisper, "It's snow!"

After I got dressed, we wrote a note to Dad and

left it on the kitchen table. The way I signed my name was so messy you could barely tell what it said. We spent all morning running around and throwing snowballs at each other, and we didn't stop till Dad called us in to have breakfast. For years Dad kept that note on the inside of the cabinet in his room, and he told me that every time Jerry and I'd go out riding he'd put that on the kitchen table as a tradition.

"Morning, little lady."

I was brought back from my memories to see Tyler looking at me. While I was absorbed in my memories, the sun had come up and the ranch had begun to stir. They had already brought in a large amount of the cows, and we were going to take them on a cattle drive to market. The other men were almost ready when I rode up on Buttercup.

"Kid, there's no way in the world you're coming with us."

I was about to yell at him when Tyler came to my rescue. "Oh yes, she is. She'll ride with me till she learns the ropes. You ready?"

"Yes, sir."

"Just follow what I do and you'll have the hang of it in no time."

That's just what I did. For most of the day we drove the cows toward the market. Our job was to round up the strays that would wander off. After I worked with him for a while, I started patrolling the other side of the herd. Every time I'd see a cow starting to wander off, I'd swing Buttercup in a wide arc and drive the cow back to the herd. By the end of the day I was bushed. They gave me the evening watch over the cows after some persuasion

115

from Tyler. You see, the evening watch was the favored one, because you could perform your watch over the cows and still get a good night's sleep. We took turns watching over the cows and took turns taking different shifts, anywhere from when we first made camp to five or six o'clock in the morning, when we'd start off again.

To keep my mind occupied as I watched over the cows, I remembered the days I first started learning to ride. Just about the time the sun was setting Tyler came over to keep me company. "How do you feel after a long day of riding?"

"Good. I'm getting paid to do what I love most."

"What's that?"

"Working with cattle and horses."

"You're fast at rounding up stay cows. They barely have time to wander off before you swing around and put them back on the right track."

"I did a lot of that when I was working with my dad and my brother."

We talked for a long time. He told me a little bit more about his family, and I told him some more about mine. When it came time for a man to take over for me, Tyler and I rode back to the fire to eat some vittles: baked beans and rehydrated beef. Just the way we did it when we were out on our range.

"Kid, have you come to your senses yet? Want to turn back?" One of the men called from the other side of the fire.

"Why on earth would I want to turn back? This is the life for me."

"You won't be saying that after two weeks on the trail."

I wasn't going to let him knock me down; not this time, not ever. Keeping my voice steady and a firm expression on my face, I responded, "Yes, I will. You can't make me back out on my love of ranching no matter how hard you try."

"Now that's not too ladylike, now is it, Joe?"

"Naw, that's not ladylike at all. I think we should teach her some manners now, don't you?"

I was about to dive over the fire and tackle them both when I felt a hand grip down on my shoulder., Tyler was standing over me, keeping me from exploding. In a stern, cold voice he said, "Leave her alone and we won't have any trouble."

I tried to twist away from his grip, yet his grip remained firm. "Tyler, leave me alone; I can fight my own battles."

"Not this way."

"But I need to show them that they can't get away with that kind of thing."

"Just go for a walk and cool off."

I wanted to argue some more, but I knew it wouldn't be any use. With clenched fists, I stood up and walked away from the fire. After I walked a ways from the fire, I tilted my head back and gazed up at the stars.

"You cooled off yet?"

"Not enough to go sit with those men."

"You know that fighting won't achieve anything except more trouble."

"That's just what my dad said."

"Did he also tell you that it takes more strength not to fight, than to fight?"

"Yes, sir."

"Just keep that in mind next time they start teasing you. If they won't leave you alone, just shout and I'll be there in a flash."

"I will. Thanks, Tyler."

"Sure, kiddo."

CHAPTER 24

For a week I rode with the men. So many times, I wanted to draw back and punch them, yet every time I almost snapped, I remembered what Tyler said. On day we came close to a small town. We were running low on supplies, so Tyler and I needed to go into town to buy some. We were about to purchase our provisions when Tyler introduced me to the store keeper, "Mr. Williams, this is my friend from the home ranch."

"Good to meet you, sir, my name's Lillian. Lillian Hartley."

Someone from behind startled me and caused me turn around.

"Hartley?! You said your name was Hartley? You don't happen to know a young man by the name of Jerry Hartley, do you?"

A man was standing there. He had a scar on his forehead, and I could tell something was wrong with his leg. I felt a chill go down my back, and the color drained from my face. Tyler saw something was wrong and said, "You okay, Lillian?"

Trying to keep my voice from shaking too much, I ignored Tyler's question and said to the young man, "How do you know my brother?"

His expression changed from a questioning look

to a look of sadness. "So, you're Jerry's little sister, Lillian Hartley? I should have known by those pure blue eyes from your dad and those broad strong shoulders that you shared with your brother."

"Yes, but how did you know I have blue eyes and broad shoulders?"

"You kidding? When Jerry, the other soldiers, and I would talk about back home, Jerry would always take out a picture of his little sister and tell about all the things you two used to do together, including many 'Once upon a time, Lillian did...' fill-in-the-blank stories. He could make us laugh; even in the hardest times he could always make us laugh. I was his best buddy to the very end."

I could see he was remembering as he looked into the emptiness.

"He really told those stories about me? How did he die?"

His voice quivered just a slight bit. "A true American hero."

"Everybody says that, but I don't believe them. There's no proof, so why should I?"

"You shouldn't blame your brother for enlisting," he said.

"He went and got himself killed, so why shouldn't I blame him?"

I could tell he was hurt by what I said.

"We were at the battle of La Drang. I'd gotten shot in the leg by the enemy fire, and I couldn't make it to safety. Jerry bounced up to pull me back to safety. He'd just gotten me there when he got shot in the back. I pulled him behind a barricade and said I was going to try to save him. He knew he'd die any minute, though, so with the last of his strength he took off his necklace and handed it to me. He asked me to give it to you. I took his hand and told him that he'd make it and he could give it to you himself, but he said it was time for him to go Home. Then he muttered a prayer, drew his last breath, and met his Redeemer face to face. His hand slipped from mine and he was gone. We were in the heat of battle and I'd just lost my best friend."

With that, he reached down, took out of his bag a couple books and Jerry's necklace, and handed them to me. "Here, these rightfully belong to you now: the journal and Bible I found at the foot of his bunk at the base; Jerry wanted you to have them."

I took them, necklace in one hand, books in the other. I looked down at the necklace in my hand which I knew all too well. It was still on the same string that it was on when he first finished it. It was an eagle, carved out of a round of wood about an inch and a half across and about a quarter-inch thick. The way he carved it, the eagle was in full flight, wings spread. The circle continued all the way around, and the eagle was connected by the tips of its wings and its talons. The color was a deep burgundy red, since he stained it. As I looked at it, I remembered how he spent hours carving it to make every last detail perfect. Then, remembering where I was, I said, "It wasn't your fault that Jerry died. No one made him save you, and it was his own choice to give his life for you."

"You're right. No one made him save me, but that's what made his sacrifice so noble. He did it out of the love he had for Jesus and people. You see, Lillian, I was not a Christian, but when your brother gave his life for me, he showed me there's more to living that what we can see

121

on the surface. A week after Jerry saved my life, I accepted Christ into my heart."

I dropped my eyes to the floor to hide the hot tears that I was sure were burning at the corners of my eyes. I turned and walked out of the store with Tyler. I didn't say much for the rest of the day.

The sun was down and I sat there, head in my hands. I had Jerry's journal opened up in front of me, and by the light of the fire I could see an old Scottish prayer that our Grandpa taught us a long time ago.

As the rain hides the stars,
as the autumn mist
hides the hills,
as the clouds veil
the blue of the sky, so
the dark happenings of my lot
hide the shining of thy face from me.
Yet, if I may hold thy hand in the darkness,
it is enough, since I know,
that though I may stumble in my going,
Thou dost not fall.

I thought about what his mindset was till the very end. I looked at the date at the top of the page. He wrote that the morning that he died; those were the last words he wrote in his beloved journal. Then I remembered that the young man said, "He said it was time for him to go Home. Then he muttered a prayer, drew his last breath, and met his Redeemer face to face." I was comforted to know that in everything, my brother was a man of God. Both his last words in his journal and the way he was last seen on earth showed that plain and clear. As I lay down on my bedroll and looked into the fire, I thought about how everyone had been right. Jerry was a true American hero, and now I had proof.

CHAPTER 25

The next morning, we continued on the drive. For the rest of the cattle drive, my endurance grew. It was all fun until Tyler got sick. One evening, Tyler wasn't feeling too well, so he hit the sack early. When I came back from washing my second pair of clothes the next morning, he was still lying there. I could tell he'd noticed my confused expression, and he said in a nasally voice, "Lillian, I've come down with the flu, so Devin's going to stay with me. Then, when I'm better, we'll ride and catch up with y'all."

"What about the cows that wander off?"

"You're fast enough to chase down all of them and still have time to relax."

There was so much more I wanted to ask, when one of the other guys called over to me, "Hey kid, you coming?"

I gave one last look to Tyler, then saddled and mounted Buttercup. As soon as we were out of hearing distance of Tyler and Jim, one of the guys called over to me, "Kid, there's something you need to get straight now that Tyler's not with us. My word goes. That means anything I tell you to do, you do it. Got it?"

In response, I chased down a cow and turned it back toward the herd.

For the entire day I chased down every cow that

dared to break away from the herd. I kept my mind occupied. I remembered my last days with Jerry; one of the last big adventures we had together was once when we were left in the big city by our dad.

He had left us to look at the trains at the station while we waited for our train pull out. Well, we had so much fun ducking in and out of all the little passage ways between the trains that we lost track of time.

"Lillian, did you know that in the old days people would hop on slow moving freight cars and ride for miles across country?"

"Yes, I knew that, remember? Dad told us about that when we learned about the Great Depression."

"Oh, that's right. Don't you think it would be so much fun to actually hop on a train and watch the miles and miles go by?"

"We're going to do that today."

"It's not the same when you are in a passenger car as when you are sitting on the edge of an open boxcar."

We walked and talked for a while when, far in the distance, I heard a man calling. "All aboard who's coming aboard! Last call for the 2:19 to Austin!"

"Jerry, that's our train! We're going to miss it!"

"Oh no we're not!" He said, grabbing my hand and beginning to run. We dodged under and jumped over anything in our way, trying to make the train. As we ran up it was beginning to move. In the back there were some empty, open boxcars. I could tell Jerry had a plan, since as soon as he saw our train, he said, "Lillian, whatever you do, keep hold of my hand and do what I say."

He wasn't running toward the passenger cars anymore; he was running right toward the boxcars. By the time we reached them, the train was moving pretty fast. Jerry knew what he was doing though, he ran my legs off. Just as he caught up with the train, he gripped my arm tightly, then reached up and grabbed a part of the boxcar opening. At the same time, he jumped and swung up into the boxcar. As soon as he was in, he swung me up, and I grabbed onto him for dear life.

"Well, Lillian, you just hopped a freight," he said with a smile. I pushed myself further back into the car, then watched the rest of the train yard rush by just feet away.

"Jerry, we're hobos now."

"Then let's sit back and enjoy the ride."

Jerry pointed things out as the world rushed by. The wind felt wonderful and everything looked so much brighter than it did from through the window.

When we got to the other end, we met our dad. He tried to look serous as he scolded us for loosing track of time and not coming back on time, yet the whole time his eyes were twinkling, and he broke into a giant smile as he took us into his arms calling us his little hobos.

The men didn't give me any more trouble until we made camp for the night. I was grooming Buttercup when I heard a voice behind me.

"Kid, go get us some water from the river to cook with," he demanded. Not turning around or saying anything, I continued grooming Buttercup. He said, in an even harsher voice, "I said, go get some water!"

When I still didn't say anything, he grabbed my shoulder and that was it--he had gone too far. In one swift motion I spun around, hooking his arm with my elbow, locking it into place. With a full fist, I threw all my weight

126

into a punch to the nose, then reared back and elbowed him right in the stomach. Knowing he'd be on me any second, I grabbed the rains with one hand. With the other I took hold of a handful of Buttercup's mane, swinging up. Taking one last look at the fire and the men, I rode away bareback into the night.

CHAPTER 26

The night was cold and dark. All I had on me was a long-sleeve button-down, jeans, and riding boots. I don't know what I thinking exactly, but when one of the men had laid their hands on me, something snapped. One thing I was sure of. I wasn't going back, not on my life. I kept riding all through the night, until my fingers were so numb that they felt like they'd fall off if I didn't warm up soon. Right when I was about to give out and stop, I saw a light far off in the distance. I knew it had to be Tyler's and Devin's, since I had just backtracked the route that we'd taken the cows that day. The sun was just peeping over the horizon when I reached the fire. I was so cold that I nearly fell off Buttercup.

Tyler helped me stand up and looked me over. "What are you doing here? Where are the other guys?"

"It was the other guys. They wouldn't leave me alone."

"Did they put their hands on you?"

When I didn't answer at first, he asked again in a more urgent voice, "Did they hurt you?"

Avoiding his eyes, I answered in a soft voice, "No, sir, they didn't have the chance to. As soon as he laid his hands on me, I reared back, elbowed him in the stomach, and rode away."

I'd never seen Tyler really angry until now. "I swear I'll kill them if they ever dare lay their hands on you again."

"No, you won't, Tyler." We turned and saw Devin standing watching us with an armload of firewood. I hadn't noticed him walk up and wondered how long he'd been listening.

"Do that and you'll just get yourself killed. Looks like Lillian fought her own battle just fine."

He'd put down the firewood, picked up a blanket, and wrapped it around my shoulders. I hugged it tight as Devin poured a cup of coffee and handed it to me. I remembered my dad's rule about coffee and paused a minute before taking a sip.

"You'll freeze to death if you don't get something hot in your body soon."

"Yes, sir."

I took a sip, and though I didn't like the taste, the hot liquid felt great running down my throat.

"Now, back to what I was saying. Lillian can fight her own battles, but just in case she needs to use anything more than her fists and elbows, we should teach her how to use one of these."

He took from his saddle a lever action rifle and propped it on his knee.

"Come on, kid, let's set up an empty tin and teach you how to shoot."

He picked up an empty bean can from their dinner the night before and set it a ways off. Then he took some ammunition from his saddlebag and loaded the gun. "Ever used one of these before?"

"Once or twice."

"So, you know how to operate and use it properly?"

"Yes, sir."

"Then let's see it," he said, handing the gun to me. I ran my hands over it, getting to know the feel of the gun. Once I was used to the weight, I raised it to my shoulder, took aim, and fired. Once I'd fired, I kept cocking the lever and firing again until I'd used all the ammunition. I was fast and clean.

"Now the question is, did you hit anything?" Tyler said.

I made sure the chamber was clear, then laid down the gun, and the three of us walked to see if I'd hit the can. When we reached the can, I thought Devin and Tyler's eyes would bulge out of their heads. I'd hit it in the center so many times there wasn't much left of it.

"Tyler, are my eyes fooling me? Didn't there used to be a tin can there?"

"Your eyes aren't fooling you unless mine are playing the same trick on me."

Turning to me, Devin said, "Where did you learn to shoot like that?"

"From my dad, mostly. Once I learned to shoot, I went on coyote patrol, keeping the population down so they couldn't make dinner out of our cows."

"Know how to use a six gun?"

"I can shoot, but I'm not as fast as I am with a rifle."

"Well, starting today that's going to change."

He went over to his saddle and took the gun belt off of the saddle horn. He brought it over, wrapped it around my waist, then buckled it at the tightest hole. Even then it hung lose. He took the pistol, made sure that it was empty, then handed it to me. I took it in my hand. It felt heavy and solid.

"Now, put it in your holster, then draw it as fast as you can on my signal."

I slipped it in the holster, planted my feet, and was ready to draw.

"Now!"

I drew and was ready to cock it. I knew I was slow, and he did too. For the next hour he worked with me, until I wasn't as fast as lightning, but faster than when I started. By the time we were done, Tyler had some breakfast sizzling in a pan on the fire. After we'd eaten breakfast, Tyler and Devin saddled their horses, and I put Buttercup's bridle on her so I was ready to ride. When we rode into town, we didn't stop at the general store, but rode right on until they slowed in front of the saloon. They dismounted and tied their horse's reigns to the hitching rail. When I hesitated, Tyler turned and said, "Don't worry, Lillian, it's safe, and you'll have both Devin and me as your personal body guards."

Assured by what he said, I dismounted and joined them. When we pushed through the batwing doors, the bartender behind the bar called to Tyler, "How're you feeling, Tyler?"

"Better, thanks, we'll be ready to pull out tomorrow morning."

"Who's this little lady you've got with you?"

"This is Lillian Hartley. Mr. Tait hired her on right before we left for the cattle drive."

By this time, the three of us were sitting on stools at the bar. "So, what can I get for you, Tyler?"

131

"I'll take a whisky and she'll take a birch beer."

I wanted to protest, until the bartender gave me a wink, then plopped a big mug down in front of me. I didn't touch the mug at first. It was my curiosity that did it. Slowly, I took hold of the mug and raised it to my lips. It tasted wonderful! It was the sweetest, most delicious soda pop I'd ever tasted. We spent the next half hour or so talking to the bartender. Once I'd finished my birch beer and Tyler and I were ready to go, we walked down main Street to the general store. While they were buying food and other supplies, I walked over to where there was a pile of newspapers. My eyes scanned the headlines and list of stories inside. I kept telling myself, "Stop looking, Lillian, stop! He's not coming home, and there's nothing you can do about it. What's done is done." Though, deep down, I knew I needed to hold on to something of my dad. And if that something was scanning the newspapers for articles about unknown soldiers that are found, then so be it.

CHAPTER 26

Over the next couple days, I rode with Tyler and Devin till we caught up with the rest of the men. We rode in a group until we reached the ranch. The first couple days back, we were mostly recovering from the long ride and getting back into the swing of things. The men had learned to leave me alone for the most part--having Tyler around really helped. About a week after we got back to the ranch, Tyler came up to me. "Lillian, you're coming with me today. Mr. Tait said there's a strip of fencing by the train track that needs to be restrung."

Tyler was coming out of the house as I slipped on my jacket.

"We'll be taking the truck, since we need to take a coil of barbed wire and some fresh fence posts."

I helped Tyler load the supplies into the back of the pickup truck, then we got in and drove to the train tracks.

The job was pretty routine. Everything went just right, until the wire snapped. I was on one end increasing the torque, and Tyler was making sure it was tight enough. Well I had tightened it too much, and just as Tyler got near it, the wire snapped. I yelled at him to get out of the way, but it was too late. The wire recoiled and hit his leg, ripping right through the denim and into his leg. By the time I got there, Tyler was on the ground. I kneeled down to look at how bad it was. It was deep and long.

"Lillian, you need to go for help. Cut over that hill and keep heading straight south, that'll lead you right to the house."

At that instant I heard a clap of thunder. Looking up, I saw darkening clouds on the horizon. I knew I didn't have time to walk back, so I came up with a better idea. Still on my knees, I unwound the barbed wire from his leg. "I have a better idea. Do you think you can make it to the truck with my help?"

"Yeah, I think so. Why?"

"Don't ask any questions, let's just get you to the truck."

I helped him up and he hobbled to the truck.

"Can you bend your wounded leg?"

"No, not much."

"Then you can ride in the bed. Hold on."

Tyler leaned on the side of the truck while I emptied the truck bed and laid my jacket down as padding. I grabbed some towels out of the cab and laid them down next to my jacket. Then I helped Tyler into the back of the tuck.

"Kid, what are you up to?"

"You'll see. Can I have the keys?"

"Why?"

"Because, I'm going to *take* you to help."

"You're darn crazy. Here you go."

He took the keys from his jean pocket and handed them to me. I climbed into the cab and started the engine. I opened the back window so I could talk to Tyler. I stared out nice and easy, since I hadn't driven my dad's truck since he'd been called up.

"Where on earth did you learn how to drive? A stick shift, moreover!"

"My dad taught me. He said it would come in handy someday, and I guess he was right," I called back, keeping my eyes on the road.

Thankfully we had the camper shell on, because I hadn't been driving two minutes when it began to rain, hard. It was coming down in sheets by the time I made it out to the road that led to the ranch. I tried to remember everything my dad had taught me to keep the truck from going into a ditch. Because of the rain, it was slow going. At last I could make out the ranch buildings in the distance. I drove the truck right up in front of the house. I shut off the engine and hopped out. I pounded on the front door, trying to imagine what I'd do if for some reason he wasn't home.

Mr. Tait came to the door. "What's wrong, Lillian?"

"It's Tyler. He's hurt, bad. He's in the back of the truck."

"Well then, let's get him inside."

He went with me to the back of the truck. Tyler had passed out because of loss of blood. We carried him inside, and Mr. Tait called to his wife what happened. She got some towels and laid them on the couch. Mr. Tait and I eased Tyler down. I was searching his face for any movement, anything at all. When I turned around, I saw a young lady standing in the doorway to the hall. I didn't recognize her, so Mr. Tait introduced her to me. "Lillian, this is my daughter, Emily. Emily, this is Lillian, the one I was telling you about."

135

I said hello, then Mrs. Tait broke in. "Dan, Tyler needs to go the emergency room, there's too much damage. I can only do so much for him."

"Alright, honey. Lillian, help me get Tyler into the back of the pickup. That'll be the safest way to get him to the hospital."

"Yes, sir." Mrs. Tait fetched some more blankets and towels. In the pouring rain she made a bed for Tyler in the back of the pickup, and then I helped Mr. Tait transfer Tyler to the bed. I tossed Mr. Tait the keys and hopped in the passenger side. He headed right for the city. I tried to keep telling myself that Tyler was going to be okay, that he wasn't going to die.

We pulled into the hospital's emergency room and Mr. Tait explained the situation to one of the doctors. They brought out a stretcher and took Tyler in. The nurse told us to wait in the waiting room. I paced around for ages. I was still in my drenched clothes, but that was the least of my worries. Mr. Tait tried to get me to sit still, but it didn't work. I ran my hand along the sweatband of my cowboy hat, trying to pass time.

Finally, after what felt like hours, a doctor came out and asked for Mr. Tait. Mr. Tait and I talked to the doctor.

"I'm afraid it's not good news. Tyler slipped into a coma from loss of blood. If you had waited much longer to bring him in, he easily could have died. The barbed wire cut the artery in the leg. He's lost a lot of blood, and his leg is in bad shape."

CHAPTER 27

I stood there shocked. "Is he going to be alright?" I said, frantically. "Is there anything that can be done, Doctor?"

"We've bandaged up his leg. All we can do now is wait. There's nothing you can do here. We'll give you a call as soon as he comes out of his coma."

"Alright. Come on, Lillian, let's go."

"We can't just leave him." My voice almost cracked.

Mr. Tait laid his hand on my shoulder. "Lillian, there's nothing we can do here. They'll call us as soon as he wakes up."

With a little more urging from Mr. Tait, I turned and followed him out to the pickup. We didn't say more than two words to each other on the ride home. When we pulled into the ranch, Mr. Tait said, "Lillian, why don't you move your things into the guest room while Tyler's away."

"Yes, sir."

I walked over to the bunkhouse and opened the door. The men turned from their poker game as I walked in.

Jim eyed me as I walked over to the bunk. "Where you been, kid? Skipping out on work?"

I clenched my teeth to keep steam from coming

out of my ears. I didn't answer; instead, I rolled up my blanket and bedroll.

"Kid, I asked you a question! Answer me! Why did you skip out on work this afternoon?"

Through clenched teeth I responded to his question. "I had better things to do."

"Yeah, sure you did. What are you doing now? Running away now that Tyler ain't here to protect you?"

"I don't need anyone to protect me."

"Is that so? Well then, I can tell the boss to stop paying Tyler to protect you."

He'd walked up so close behind me that I could feel his breath on the back of my neck. This time I wasn't going to let him touch me. I spun around and punched him right in the stomach. The fight was on. The other men moved the table out of the way and we laid into each other. I remembered what Jerry had taught me and I used my size to my advantage. The men all sat on their bunks so the floor was clear.

I was so focused on the fight that I didn't notice the door open and Mr. Tait come in. "Break it up! You heard me, break it up!"

He grabbed the back of my shirt and jerked me to my feet. "Jim, you stay here and cool off. Lillian, you're coming with me."

He didn't let go of me until we were outside. We walked over to the corral fence where he leaned on the top rail and looked out into the setting sun. "Well? What do you have to say for yourself?"

I didn't respond at first, just looked out at the sun shimmering off of the wet ground. I didn't know what to say. It was my fault, but how could I tell him that? He could sense my hesitation, so he continued, "How'd it start?"

"He was teasing me again. I guess I'd just had enough. If it wasn't for Tyler, I'd have fought Jim the first day I came here."

"You can't let him get to you."

"I know, I just was tired of him thinking he could push me around like that. I wanted him to see that I didn't need Tyler to fight my battles for me."

"Pride like that could get yourself killed."

I knew a scolding when I got one. He did them just like my dad, dropping them into the conversation.

"Yes, sir."

"Let me look you over."

He turned and looked me up and down. I had a bloody lip and a black eye. I'd given Jim much worse. If Mr. Tait hadn't broke up the fight when he did, I probably would have won.

"You're not too bad. Get your things from the bunkhouse and head inside. This time, go directly to your bunk, get your things, and come out. No fighting. Period."

"Yes, sir."

I turned and walked back to the bunkhouse. Once I'd packed up my belongings, I went back to the house. When I entered, Emily was sitting at the kitchen table with Mr. and Mrs. Tait.

"What happened to you?" Emily asked.

"Jim and I had a bit of a disagreement. I'll be fine. Any word on Tyler?"

Mrs. Tait looked up from her tea. "No, not yet. What happened to you?"

"I was caught in a bit of a fistfight. I'll be fine."

"That bloody lip and black eye tells me otherwise. Come over here and let me see how bad it is."

"Yes, ma'am."

I walked over to where she was sitting, She stood up and carefully touched the edge of my eye. I flinched at the pain and pulled back.

I was turning to go to the guestroom when Mr. Tait picked up the phone. "Hello? … Yes, this is Dan Tait …Really! … Alright, we'll be right there. Bye."

Mr. Tait hung up the phone, "Lillian, I want you to stay here. I need to go in and check in on Tyler. Doc said he's coming out of his coma."

"Can't I come with you?"

"No, I don't want Tyler to see you like this. Stay here and get cleaned up. I'll be back soon."

"Yes sir."

After Mr. Tait left, Mrs. Tait took me to the bathroom and tended the cuts and scrapes on my face.

Emily came in and asked, "What kind of girl gets into a fistfight?"

"I do."

"You're not much of a girl, then. First you drive a truck, now this! A real girl would have walked away from the fight."

I felt a prickle run down my back. I told myself to stay calm and not to pay any mind to Emily. But then she continued. "A real girl wouldn't come and work on a cattle ranch. She'd be home growing up with her family, not working in the dirt with a bunch of filthy cattle hands. You can't be more than what? Fifteen? You should still be in school, not working full time away from home. What kind of girl are you? You should just go home and be with your

140

family where you belong."

Every part of me wanted to yell at her, to tell her I didn't have a home or family or anything. Instead, I knew what I had to do. I asked Mrs. Tait for a pen and paper, then I headed out to Buttercup in the barn. In the barn I began writing,

Dear Mr. Tait,

After the past weeks working on the ranch, I've come to the realization that I don't belong here. I'm sorry for the short notice, but I am resigning from my post on this ranch. Please tell your daughter I'm the kind of girl who knows when to walk away from a fight and when to face it head on. Again, I'm sorry for the short notice.

Sincerely,

Lillian Hartley

I folded up the note and placed it in my shirt pocket. I had a certain sadness as I saddled up Buttercup. I kept my eyes on what I was doing as I walked to the guest room and packed up my few belongings, leaving my note on the pillow.

I turned to leave when Mrs. Tait stood in the doorway, "And where do you think you're going, young lady? Dan asked you to stay in here until Tyler gets back to the ranch. We were talking about it, and we've decided you'll stay in the guest room from now on."

"And I would respect that decision if I was working here anymore. But I'm not, I'm resigning, and no offence, ma'am, but you can't stop me. Now, if you'll excuse me, I have many miles to travel before making camp."

She didn't say anything, she just stood aside and watched me leave. As I rode away from the ranch, I felt something inside me fall. The further away I rode the

141

worse I felt, especially about leaving Tyler without saying goodbye. The more I thought about it, the more knew what I had to do. I rode in the direction of the hospital. I tied Buttercup behind the hospital and made my way around to the front. Entering the hospital, I used my guest pass from earlier and headed to Tyler's room. I stopped in the doorway when I heard Mr. Tait and Tyler talking.

"You mean she just resigned? Just like that? She didn't even talk to you in person? That's not like her."

"I know, Tyler. Joanne just called and said she left a note in the guest room. I don't know what's gotten into her--first the fight, then this."

"But Dan, where's she going to go? You know she doesn't have any family left alive. I've seen her so mad that I was sure smoke would come out of her ears, but she didn't quit. At least she would have come back and said goodbye. And with my leg the way it is I can't go after her. I can't figure out why she'd do such a thing."

I stood there, wanting to leave, yet knowing I had to stay. So, taking a deep breath, I walked in.

"Lillian! You came back!"

"Yeah, Tyler, I came back. I couldn't leave without saying goodbye."

"But why'd you leave in the first place?"

"Because I can't change what the war's done to my family…and to me."

"That's not an answer, young lady." Mr. Tait said in a low voice.

"Yes, sir. The truth is that I'm tired of being treated like a little kid, first by the men, and now Emily."

"Emily?"

"Yes sir, Emily. She said that a real girl wouldn't

142

have fought and that she'd be home with her family, not roughnecking on a ranch. It was too much, and that's why I can't stay here anymore."

"I'll make you a deal. I'll talk to Emily if you give me your word you'll stick around another week. If you still feel this way at the end of the week, you can go."

"Okay, will do."

"Lillian, I heard you whooped Jim something awful. You think you taught him a lesson?"

"Don't encourage her, Tyler. She's hurt bad enough as it is, don't make it worse."

"Yes, boss."

CHAPTER 28

Before long Tyler was up and hopping again. Soon after we got back to the ranch, Dan fired Jim and gave the other men strict warnings. He also told me I was no longer allowed to board in the bunkhouse, but I'd have to stay in the guest room from then on. The days turned in to weeks and the weeks into months. I opened a bank account at a local bank, and Mr. Tait took me in as his daughter as much as his ranch hand. We had countless evening walks and long talks. I thought my life was as perfect as it could get after what 'Nam had done me.

I'd been there about two years when the telegram came. Tyler was being drafted to go to Vietnam.

About that same time, I got an unusual letter in the mail. It had no return address, and I couldn't make out the postmark. All it said was, "I'm coming home."

It was a really hard day when he left the ranch for the last time. I walked out to say goodbye for the last time. "Listen, Tyler, and while you're over there, keep an eye out for my dad, will ya?"

"Sure, kiddo. You take care of yourself, okay?"

"Okay."

With that he turned and walked down the drive to the road to catch a ride to town. I watched him until he went out of sight. I knew I had to finish the day, though, so I saddled up and began to ride to check the fence.

I was out all day; the sun was setting when I made it back to the ranch. As I rode up, a man was standing talking to Mr. Tait. He had his back to me, and his voice sounded faintly familiar.

"Hello, Mr. Tait, I'm done for the day. Everything checks out."

Without turning his head, the man that Mr. Tait called "Davey" said, "I'd know that voice anywhere. Wait, don't tell me, you've got long blond hair pulled back into two braids, you've got sky blue eyes that are as sharp as a hawk, and you've got a scar approximately two inches long crossways on the inside of your left forearm."

A shiver ran down my back, and I didn't want to get my hopes up,--could it be? Could it really be...?

"How'd...how'd you know?" My voice quivered the slightest bit.

The man turned around, raised his head, and looked me straight in the eye. "Because I know you, Lil."

"DAD!!!"

I just about jumped off Buttercup and ran to him. He caught me in a bear hug and I couldn't believe it. It was my dad!!!

Mr. Tait stood by chuckling. "Davey, I guess you already know my youngest ranch hand, Lillian."

"I guess so," my dad said, laughing.

I had so many questions. "How, Dad? I thought you were dead years ago. How do you know Mr. Tait?"

"Slow down, Lil, I'll explain everything in time. For now, let's go take care of Buttercup."

An hour later we were sitting around the dining room table having supper. I turned to my dad and asked,

"So how'd you do it? How'd you go from Missing in Action to showing up on the ranch I just happened to be working on?"

"Why are you so surprised? I sent you a letter telling you I was coming home," he said with a chuckle.

"So that was from you!"

"Yes, that was from me. To answer your original question, I was captured by the Viet Cong and was in captivity for two years, then was rescued by the Marines. When I made it back to the States, I went to the Johnsons' to get you and you weren't there."

"I'm sorry, Dad, I…I just couldn't stay there anymore."

"I understand. Back to my story. When Will heard I was your father, he took me aside and told me where you went."

"I sent Will a letter, told him I was safe and what ranch I'm working on."

"When I heard that it was Dan's ranch, I gave him a call and told him I'd like to buy enough cattle and take his prize ranch hand."

"But Dad, why do you need the cattle?"

"Because we're going home."

But those who wait on the LORD
Shall renew their strength;
They shall mount up with wings like eagles,
They shall run and not be weary,
They shall walk and not faint.
Isaiah 40:31

EPILOGUE

The sun was just setting on the Vietnam Memorial as Lillian Hartley stood in silence looking at one name in particular. It had been twenty years since the day that her brother gave his life in Vietnam. As she stood looking at her brother's name engraved in the stone, a man came up and quietly asked, "Do you know someone on this wall?"

"Yes, a hero. A hero who gave his life so another could live. You?"

"I know many men with their names on this wall. I fought in Vietnam and was injured at the battle of La Drang. I saw things that no one should ever have to experience--men laying down their lives for a friend, for freedom. My best friend gave his life for me at the battle of La Drang. His name was Jerry, Jerry Hartley. Ever since they opened this memorial, I come here on the day he died to honor my fallen brother."

"Jerry Hartley was my brother."

"You're not Lillian?"

"Yes, I'm Lillian Hartley."

"Well, you're certainly not the little girl that Jerry used to talk about. But you look just like he described."

At that moment a little boy ran up. "Hey, Dad, are you almost done? Mom said we need to get home so she can tend to little Lillian."

"Sure, just one second, Jerry."

147

As soon as I heard those names, I turned and looked at the boy "Jerry? Lillian?"

"Yup. Jerry's my name, and Lillian's my little sister."

I turned to the man with a queer expression on my face.

He read me like a book. "I never forgot the man who saved me over there. When Mary-Jane and I settled down and had our first boy, I couldn't think of a better name than Jerry."

"Dad, who is this woman?"

"Jerry, this is Lillian."

Jerry turned to me with big round eyes. "You're Lillian Hartley!"

"Yes, I am."

"My dad told me so many stories about you and your brother. How your brother saved his life and how he showed him the Light found in Jesus, but I never thought I'd actually get to meet you."

I remembered that I still had Jerry's necklace in my pocket from years ago. I felt his dog tags around my neck and knew what I had to do. I walked over to where the boy was standing, took the necklace, and laid it around his neck, saying, "Jerry, I want you to do something for me. I want you to wear this necklace, and whenever you look at it, I want you to remember my brother's story. When Lillian grows up, I want you to tell it to her and keep the story alive. Never, never forget: Freedom isn't free."

Made in the USA
Monee, IL
24 July 2020